THE LITTLE
BIG BOOK OF

Birds

Edited by
Natasha Tabori Fried
and **Lena Tabori**

THE LITTLE
BIG BOOK OF

Birds

INTRODUCTION BY KENN KAUFMAN

Welcome Books
New York • San Francisco

Published in 2007 by Welcome Books
An imprint of Welcome Enterprises, Inc.
6 West 18th Street, New York, NY 10011
Tel: 212-989-3200; Fax: 212-989-3205
www.welcomebooks.com

Publisher: Lena Tabori
Designer: Jon Glick, mouse+tiger
Project Manager: Natasha Tabori Fried
Assistant Editor: Maren Elizabeth Gregerson
Editorial Assistant: Kara Mason
Special thanks to Mary Vanderford for her expertise and
enthusiasm for this project.

Copyright © 2007 Welcome Enterprises, Inc.
Introduction © 2007 Kenn Kaufman

Additional credits and copyright information
available on page 352.

Library of Congress Cataloging-in-Publication Data

The little big book of birds / edited by Natasha Tabori
Fried. -- 1st ed.
     p. cm.
  ISBN-13: 978-1-59962-023-7
1. Birds. 2. Bird watching. I. Fried, Natasha.
QL676.L57 2006
  598--dc22

                                          2006033952

ISBN–10: 1-59962-023-5
ISBN–13: 978-1-59962-023-7

Printed in China

First Edition

10 9 8 7 6 5 4 3 2 1

Contents

BIRD POETRY

BIRDWATCHING 101

BIRDWATCHING AROUND THE WORLD

FAMOUS BIRDER BIOGRAPHIES

INTRODUCTION

A POPULAR THEME in works of fiction involves the concept of parallel worlds. There is something appealing about the idea that there might be alternate worlds, parallel to our own, near at hand but known to only a few. The beings described as inhabiting these fantasy realms are somewhat like us, but different enough to be interesting. They excite our imaginations and make us more aware of the possibilities in our own lives.

It's no surprise that the idea of a secret world should be popular. The surprise comes when we realize that such a world actually exists. All over the Earth, starting right outside our windows, is the amazing world of birds. Wild birds are more varied than the residents of Oz or Wonderland or Narnia, more astonishing than leprechauns, easier to see than fairies or elves, and, I suspect, as beautiful as angels. Self-sufficient in their own realm, birds don't care whether we notice them or not. But if we do, they can enrich our experience of life every day.

One of the most delightful things about the world of birds is that it can be approached in so many different ways. Passing through the looking-glass may have been Alice's only option for gaining access to Wonderland, but we can contemplate birds from almost any direction.

It's possible to view birds from a purely scientific perspective. Even the task of classifying and naming all the birds is not yet completed— species new to science are still being discovered, after all—and once a bird is named, there are still innumerable questions to answer about

its biology and behavior. At the opposite extreme, it's possible to look at birds from a purely artistic viewpoint, without any regard for their names or any scientific fact. It's also possible to combine these seemingly disparate elements. A surprising number of ornithologists have also been painters of birds, so that *scientist-artist* has not been a rare designation in this field.

Birds can be pursued in the library. There is a rich tradition of poetry about avian subjects; the tradition of prose is every bit as rich and even more varied. Essays range from descriptive nature writing to works of philosophy, allegory, or humor, with birds being used to symbolize practically anything. Literary birdwatching is so rewarding that I have known a few people who read avidly about feathered creatures for months or even years before it occurred to them to go outside and look at birds in real life.

Perhaps most surprising is the fact that birding can be a sport. More than 900 species have shown up in North America—something like 10,000 worldwide—and some folks are drawn to the challenge of finding as many of those as possible. Keeping lists of the birds that one has identified provides a way of keeping score, and birders may compete to see who can check off the most species in one state, or one day, or one year, or one lifetime. It's only a game, but it can be immensely fun. At the opposite extreme, millions of people gain profound pleasure from simply watching birds in their backyards, appreciating the color and song and life that these wild creatures always bring to their surroundings. This appreciation can lead us to another approach, perhaps the highest one: that of the conservationist, ensuring that birds and their habitats will survive for future generations to enjoy.

I was fortunate to have become enthralled with birds at the age of six, and to have pursued them by all of the avenues just mentioned. I have done paintings of birds and have taken part in scientific studies, raced around checking off birds on my list and then spent hours in quiet observation, read great literature and poetry about birds and then tried to write my own. The pursuit of avian life has taken me into wild and beautiful places on all seven continents. Birds even led me to fall in love. I met my wife, Kim, when I went to speak at a nature festival, and literally the first thing we did together was to go birdwatching. The second thing we did was have a snowball fight, but that's another story.

As one who appreciates birds from every angle, I'm thrilled to introduce *The Little Big Book of Birds*. Lena Tabori and Natasha Tabori Fried, renowned for their brilliant work in publishing and editing, have assembled a wonderful collection of writing and artwork that celebrates the best of birding. Here you will find everything from facts to folklore, from practical advice to hilarious satire, from profiles of ornithologists to evocative poetry and prose. Whether you read the book from cover to cover or dip into it here and there for inspiring gems, I hope it will enhance your awareness of this parallel world of birds that brings so much wonder and beauty to our own world.

KENN KAUFMAN

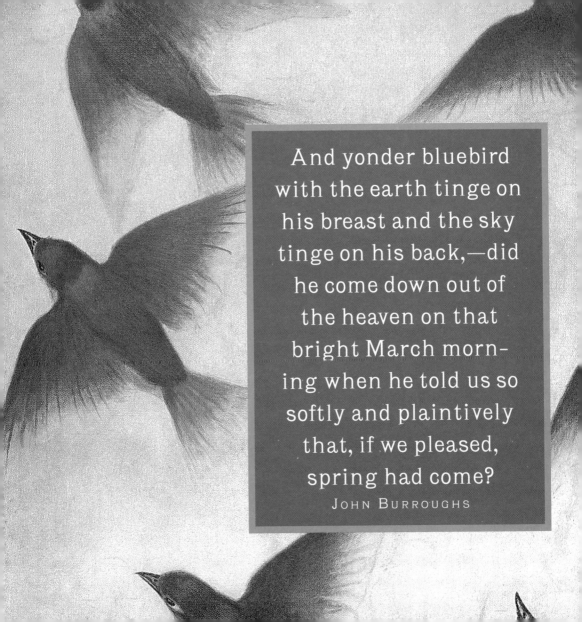

And yonder bluebird with the earth tinge on his breast and the sky tinge on his back,—did he come down out of the heaven on that bright March morning when he told us so softly and plaintively that, if we pleased, spring had come?

JOHN BURROUGHS

SPRING IS A RUSH SEASON ON ANY FARM. On this farm of ours spring becomes an almost impossible season because of the songbirds, which arrive just as everything else is getting under way and which have to be identified. They couldn't pick a more inconvenient time.

I say they have to be identified—we never used to identify songbirds, we used to lump them and listen to them sing. But my wife, through a stroke of ill fortune, somehow got hold of a book called *A Field Guide to the Birds— Including All Species Found in Eastern North America*, by Roger Tory Peterson,

FROM SONGBIRDS
BY E. B. WHITE

and now we can't settle down to any piece of work without being interrupted by a warbler trying to look like another warbler and succeeding admirably.

The birds have been here a couple of weeks now, and we are getting farther and farther behind with everything. I simply haven't time to stop what I am doing every fifteen seconds to report a white eye-ring and a yellow rump-patch, and neither has my wife. Take this morning, for instance. Our home roars and boils and seethes with activity. Upstairs is German measles. In the cellar is a water pump that has gone into a running fit. Outside,

a truck is noisily trying to back up to the woodshed door to deliver
a couple of cords of dry wood for us to spring out on. In the
shop somebody is hammering away, making a blackout frame for
the next raid. In the back kitchen the set tubs are in operation,
coping with a week's wash. In the front study my wife's typewriter
is going like the devil, trying to catch a mail with something or
other of an editorial nature. Overhead a plane grumbles and
threatens and heads out to sea. Here in the living room, where I
choose to work because it is the nerve center of the whole place
and thus enables me to keep in touch with life without moving
out of my chair, I am busy with the electric literary life of a pent-
up agriculturalist, such as it is. Lambs jump and dance in the
barnyard, waiting for the gate to swing open so they can get at the
lambkill; tiny broccoli and tomato and cabbage and lettuce plants
struggle desperately upward in flats in the south window waiting to
be transplanted into the cold frame; two hundred and seventy-two
chicks romp in the brooder house in search of trouble; the wind
blows, the bushes creak against the shutters, the sun shines, the
radio plays for the measles, and the whole place has the eleventh-
hour pulsation of a defense factory. On top of everything there
are these indistinguishable little birds crying for our attention,

FROM SONGBIRDS

flaunting an olive-green spot that looks yellow, a yellow stripe that looks gray, a gray breast that looks cinnamon, a cinnamon tail that looks brown.

This morning at breakfast my wife seemed tired and discouraged. I thought perhaps it was the measles upstairs (which we had wrongly identified, at first, as a boil in the ear). "Do you know," she said after a while, "that the fox sparrow can easily be mistaken for the hermit thrush? They are about the same size, and they both have a red tail in flight."

"They don't if you look the other way," I replied, wittily. But she was not comforted. She thumbed restlessly through *A Field Guide* (she carries it with her from room to room this season) and settled down among the grosbeaks, finches, sparrows, and buntings while I went back among the smoked bacon, blackberry jam, toast, and coffee.

"My real trouble is," she continued, "that I learn the birds pretty well one year, but then the next year comes and I have to learn them all again. I think probably the only way really to learn them is to go out with a bird person. That would be the only way."

"You wouldn't like a bird person," I replied.

"I mean a sympathetic bird person."

"You don't know a sympathetic bird person."

"I knew a Mr. Knollenberg once," said my wife wistfully, "who was always looking for a difficult finch."

She admitted, however, that the problem of the birds was virtually insoluble. Even the chickadee, it turns out, plays a dirty trick on us all. Everybody knows a chickadee, and in winter the chickadees are our constant companions. For nine months of the year the chickadee announces himself plainly, so that any simpleton can tell him; but in spring the fraudulent little devil gives a phony name. In spring, when love hits him, he goes around introducing himself as Phoebe. According to the author of *Field Guide* he whistles the name Phoebe, whereas the Phoebe doesn't whistle it but simply *says* it. Still, it's a dishonest trick, and I resent it when I'm busy.

Mr. Peterson, the author of the *Guide*, has made a manly attempt to enable us to identify birds, but the attempt (in my case) is pitiful. He says of the Eastern Winter Wren (*Nannus hiemalis hiemalis*): it "frequents mossy tangles, ravines, brushpiles." That, I don't doubt, is true of the Eastern Winter Wren; but it is also true of practically every bird here except the chimney swift and the herring gull. Our whole country is just one big mossy tangle. Any bird you meet is suspect, but they can't all be Eastern Winter Wrens.

The titmice, the wrens, the thrushes, the nuthatches, the finches are bad enough, but when Mr. Peterson comes to helping me, or even my wife, with the warblers his efforts are indeed laughable. There are dozens of warblers, many of them barely visible to the naked eye. To distinguish them from one another is like trying to distinguish between two bits of dust dancing in a shaft of sunlight. Of the Chestnut-sided Warbler Mr. Peterson says: "*Adults in spring:*—Easily identified by the *yellow* crown and the chestnut sides. The only other bird with *chestnut* sides, the Bay-breast, has a chestnut throat and a dark crown, thus appearing quite dark-headed. Autumn birds are quite different—greenish above and white below, with a white eye-ring and two wing-bars. Adults usually retain some of the chestnut. The lemon-colored shade of green, in connection with the white under parts, is sufficient for recognition." Well, it is sufficient for recognition if you happen to be standing, or lying, directly under a Chestnut-sided Warbler in the fall of the year and can remember not to confuse the issue with "adults in spring" or with the Bay-breast at *any* season—specially the *female* Bay-breast in spring, which is rather dim and indistinct, the way all birds look to me when they are in a hurry (which they almost always are) or when I am. A hurried man trying to identify a hurried bird is palpably a ridiculous situation.

Even the author of the *Guide* admits, in places, that a bird spotter is in for real trouble. The Sycamore Warbler, he says, is almost identical with the Yellow-throated Warbler, but might be distinguished "at extremely short range" by the lack of any yellow between the eye and the bill. It helps some though if you can remember which side of the Alleghenies you are on. I try to keep that in mind always.

The thing that amuses me about songbirds in our amazing springtime is the way my wife takes her troubles out on the birds themselves, who are, in a sense, innocent enough. She is puzzled and annoyed at her inability to master, in a few crowded weeks, the amazing intricacies of bird markings—made even more difficult because we sent our binoculars to England year before last to help in the defense of the British Isles. A little while ago I heard her pause for a fleeting moment at a window as she was passing by and heard her mutter peevishly: "There goes one of those damned little Yellow Palm Warblers." Then she added, in a barely audible whisper, "I guess."

Never Again Would Birds' Song Be the Same

By Robert Frost

He would declare and could himself believe
That the birds there in all the garden round
From having heard the daylong voice of Eve
Had added to their own an oversound,
Her tone of meaning but without the words.
Admittedly an eloquence so soft
Could only have had an influence on birds
When call or laughter carried it aloft.
Be that as may be, she was in their song.
Moreover her voice upon their voices crossed
Had now persisted in the woods so long
That probably it never would be lost.
Never again would birds' song be the same.
And to do that to birds was why she came.

He Said She Said:
A Mnemonics Birdsong Cheat Sheet

Red-eyed Vireo . . . *Here I am. Look at me. I'm up here!*

Yellow-throated Vireo . . . *Helen, Helen! Come here!*

White-throated Sparrow . . . *Old Sam Peabody, Peabody, Peabody!*
OR *Oh sweet Canada, Canada, Canada!*

Carolina Wren . . . *Teakettle, teakettle, teakettle!*

Barred Owl . . . *Who cooks for you? Who cooks for you-all?*

California Quail . . . *Chi-ca-go!*

Olive-sided Flycatcher . . . *Quick! Three beers!*

Black-throated Blue Warbler . . . *I am so lay-zee!*

Yellow Warbler . . . *Sweet, sweet, I'm so sweet!*

Indigo Bunting . . . *Fire! Fire! Where? Where? There! There! Put it out!*
Put it out! OR *What? What? Where? Where? Here! Here! See it! See it!*

Eastern Towhee . . . *Drink your tea!*

Golden-crowned Sparrow . . . *Oh dear me!*

Eastern Meadowlark . . . *Spring of the year!*

Prothonotary Warbler . . .
Sweet! Sweet! Sweet! Sweet! Sweet!

Warbling Vireo . . . *If I see it, I can seize it,*
and I'll squeeze it,
till it squir-r-r-rts.

American Robin . . . *Cheerup,*
cheerily, cheerily.

Eastern Bluebird . . . *Cheer, cheerful, charmer.*

Tufted Titmouse . . .
Peter, Peter, Peter.

White-breasted Nuthatch . . . *Yank yank.*

Chestnut-sided Warbler . . .
Please please pleased to meetcha.

Song Sparrow . . . *Maids, maids, maids,*
put on your teakettle, kettle, kettle.

Gray Catbird . . . *Meeeow.*

Northern Cardinal . . . *Purty, purty, purty.*

Black-throated Green Warbler . . . *Trees, trees, murmuring trees.*
OR *Zay, zay, zay, zoo, zee.*

A FEW BIRDS THAT SAY THEIR NAME:

Phoebe

Peewee

Blue Jay (says *jay*)

Whippoorwill

25

A LISTENER'S GUIDE TO THE BIRDS

By E. B. White

Wouldst know the lark?

Then hark!

Each natural bird

Must be seen *and* heard.

The lark's "Tee-ee" is a tinkling entreaty,

But it's not always "Tee-ee"—

Sometimes it's "Tee-titi."

    So watch yourself.

Birds have their love-and-mating song,

Their warning cry, their hating song;

Some have a night song, some a day song,

26

A lilt, a tilt, a come-what-may song;
Birds have their careless bough and teeter song
And, of course, their Roger Tory Peter song.

The studious ovenbird (pale pinkish legs)
Calls, "Teacher, teacher, teacher!"
The chestnut-sided warbler begs
To see Miss Beecher.
    "I wish to see Miss Beecher."
(Sometimes interpreted as "Please please please ta
    meetcha.")

The redwing (frequents swamps and marshes)
Gurgles, "Konk-la-reeee,"
Eliciting from the wood duck
The exclamation "Jeeee!"
    (But that's the *male* wood duck, remember.
    If it's his wife you seek,
    Wait till you hear a distressed "Whoo-eek!")

Nothing is simpler than telling a barn owl from a veery:

One says, "Kschh!" in a voice that is eerie,

The other says, "Vee-ur," in a manner that is breezy.

    (I told you it was easy.)

On the other hand, distinguishing between the veery

And the olive-backed thrush

Is another matter. It couldn't be worse.

The thrush's song is similar to the veery's

Only it's the reverse.

Let us suppose you hear a bird say, "Fitz-bew,"

The things you can be sure of are two:

First, the bird is an alder flycatcher (*Empidonax traillii*

    traillii);

Second, you are standing in Ohio—or, as some people

    call it, O-hee-o—

Because, although it may come as a surprise to you,

The alder flycatcher, in New York or New England,

    does not say, "Fitz-bew,"

It says, "Wee-bé-o."

"Chu-chu-chu" is the note of the harrier,

Copied, of course, from our common carrier.

The osprey, thanks to a lucky fluke,

Avoids "Chu-chu" and cries, "Chewk, chewk!"

    So there's no difficulty there.

The chickadee likes to pronounce his name;

It's extremely helpful and adds to his fame.

But in the spring you can get the heebie-jeebies

Untangling chickadees from phoebes.

The chickadee, when he's all afire,

Whistles, "Fee-bee," to express desire.

He should be arrested and thrown in jail

For impersonating another male.

    (There's a way you can tell which bird is which,

    But just the same, it's a nasty switch.)

Our gay deceiver may fancy-free be

But he never does fool a female phoebe.

Oh, sweet the random sounds of birds!

The old-squaw, practicing his thirds;

The distant bittern, driving stakes,

The lonely loon on haunted lakes;

The white-throat's pure and tenuous thread—

They go to my heart, they go to my head.

How hard it is to find the words

With which to sing the praise of birds!

Yet birds, when *they* get singing praises,

Don't lack for words—they know some daisies:

    "Fitz-bew,"

    "Konk-la-reeee,"

    "Hip-three-cheers,"

    "Onk-a-lik, ow-owdle-ow,"

    "Cheedle cheedle chew,"

And dozens of other inspired phrases.

BIRD IS THE WORD:
THE LANGUAGE OF BIRDING

Every hobby and field has its own vernacular, and birdwatching is no exception. If you've ever found yourself on a local nature walk trying to look up "LBJ" in your field guide or searching your skin when a friend remarks, "That's another tick"—well then, this glossary is for you.

Bins: Binoculars.

Birder: Anyone between a twitcher and a dude (see below).

BOP: Bird of prey.

Crippler: A rare and beautiful bird that performs well and sticks around, often "crippling" the pace of your day.

Dip out (or dip): To miss seeing a bird that you were looking for.

Dude: A British term for a casual birder—one typically out more for a nice walk in the woods than for the birds.

Eight-Hundred Club: American birders so wealthy that they can devote all their time to traveling the world simply to add a bird to their list. This is in contrast with most birders, who must continue their daily grind just so they can take a birding weekend to the best garbage dumps in their tristate area.

Grip off (or grip): To see a bird that other birders missed by leaving early . . . and then boast about it to their faces.

Jizz: The overall impression given by the shape, movement, and behavior of a species rather than any particular feature.

LBJ: Little brown job. With so many birds that are small, brown, and nondescript, it can be difficult to correctly identify them. Calling a bird an LBJ makes you sound like you know what you are talking about, even if you don't.

Lifer: A species that you have never seen before.

Mega: A bird for which you'd bail on your sister's wedding ceremony—or maybe your own—if you heard it had been spotted in the area.

Pish: A sibilant noise made to attract birds. **Pishing out** is what happens when birds respond to your pish.

Purple patch: A golden, seemingly touched-by-the-birding-gods spot where rare birds are often seen.

Sibe: A bird from Siberia (usually applied to rare migrants).

Stringer: A birder who is known for **stringing**—or misidentifying a common bird for a rarer one—more often than is acceptable, just to boost his or her list or reputation.

Suppressor: This is not a title a birder wants. A suppressor keeps information about a rare bird sighting secret so that no one else can see it or add it to their list.

Tick: A species that is new to any of your lists—life, year, country, and so on.

Twitcher: A British term for an obsessive birder who searches out rare birds to add to his or her list. The verb **to twitch** refers to going out specifically to see a particular reported rarity.

Usual suspects: The list of species expected at your birding location.

Yabow: That person in your birding habitat (be it bird sanctuary or parking lot) who is not a birder and thereby unknowingly scares all the birds off with the *Saturday Night Fever* ring tone on his or her cell phone.

In Acadia National Park, Maine, birders can enjoy more than 270 species. Check out the view of nesting Peregrine Falcons near Champlain Mountain, watch hawks soar over Bar Harbor from Cadillac Mountain, or enjoy Mount Desert's Wonderland Trail, a haven for nesting land birds.

Birding in the Northeast

For birders who enjoy a good hike, Mount Katahdin, Maine, is a wonderful place to explore. The mountain's four different vegetation zones attract a diverse group of birds, including mergansers, thrushes, raptors, and woodpeckers.

Hammonasset Beach State Park offers Connecticut birders excellent habitat variety within a small area, ranging from tidal marshes to grassy fields to young forests. Take the Willard Island Trail to hear a range of songbirds and the Piping Plover, or follow the boardwalk to see waterfowl and Black-headed Gulls.

If you are in Delaware during October or November, head to Bombay Hook National Wildlife Refuge for one of the largest concentrations of migrating Snow Geese in the United States—often better than 150,000!

Maine is only state that offers boat tours specializing in viewing the Atlantic Puffin. In the early 1900s, there was only one pair of Atlantic Puffins left below the Canadian border, but thanks to protective lighthouse owners (and later, Project Puffin), the birds have survived and now live on four islands off the coast.

Parker River National Wildlife Refuge in Massachusetts was established in 1942 as a resting, feeding, and nesting habitat for migrating waterfowl, songbirds, and shorebirds. This 4,662 acre refuge attracts more than 300 species. Go in March to see the American Woodcock begin its courtship flights, or in September to see the migrating monarch butterflies.

Cape May on the southern tip of New Jersey organizes events year-round for birders both amateur and professional. With more than 400 species sighted, join in for the Official Hawk Watch every autumn (the count totaled 60,000 in 2005), or get a team together to compete in the World Series of Birding.

If you'd like a more relaxed day of birding in New Jersey, try the Edwin B. Forsythe National Wildlife Refuge. Here an 8-mile drive brings you to key birding spots and several observation towers.

Think a park that attracts 25 million people a year would be bad for birding? Think again. New York City's Central Park has 275-plus species, including its very own favorite couple, Pale Male and Lola, two Red-tailed Hawks who have made their nest across the street on Fifth Avenue.

While in Central Park, bring the kids to Belvedere Castle, where you can pick up a Discovery Kit backpack with binoculars, a guidebook, maps, and sketching materials to aid in your nature appreciation day.

If hawks interest you, head straight for Pennsylvania's Hawk Mountain Sanctuary, the world's first refuge for predatory birds. Staff and volunteers are on hand to help you spot and learn about the birds. Stop in to see the exhibits in the visitor center before you hike the mile to the official count site—with a 180-degree view—North Lookout. Between August and December 2005, the count of predatory birds was more than 18,000, including Sharp-shinned, Cooper's, and Broad-winged Hawks.

Presque Isle State Park is a 3,200-acre sandy peninsula along Lake Erie in Pennsylvania that offers birds (and those who love them) six different ecological zones, including beaches, swamps, forests, and croplands. Don't miss the Scarlet Tanagers or Yellow-bellied Sapsuckers.

Oriole
By Edgar Fawcett

How falls it, oriole, thou has come to fly
In tropic splendor through our Northern sky?
At some glad moment was it nature's choice
To dower a scrap of sunset with a voice?
Or did some orange tulip, flaked with black,
In some forgotten garden, ages back,
Yearning toward Heaven until its wish was heard,
Desire unspeakably to be a bird?

Roger Tory Peterson

ROGER TORY PETERSON, a naturalist, ornithologist, and artist, was one of the most influential people of the 20th-century environmental movement. He was born August 28, 1908, in Jamestown, New York, to working-class immigrant parents. Growing up, there were ample opportunities for young Peterson to enjoy and learn about nature, but it is his seventh-grade teacher who is credited with his immense interest in birds and wildlife. She encouraged her class to participate in a Junior Audubon Club, and Peterson immediately became entranced by birds and their habitats. As he observed and identified each species, he made elaborate sketches. His abilities to paint and sketch birds accurately quickly improved, creating a desire to pursue a career as an artist.

Peterson moved to New York City after graduating from high school in 1927. There he enrolled in the Art Students League, then continued his education at the National Academy of Design until 1931. During this time, his interest in birds grew, and he was fortunate enough to be able to meet many of the leading ornithologists of the time. In

turn, Peterson was able to share his joy in birdwatching with the younger generation when he became a science and art teacher at the Rivers School in Brookline, Massachusetts.

In 1934, Roger Tory Peterson achieved what is considered his most noted accomplishment—his first book, *A Field Guide to Birds*. Before its publication, there was some doubt as to whether he could actually persuade people to go birdwatching, but that doubt was quickly pushed aside as his guide sold out its first printing of 2,000 copies in one week. To this day, *A Field Guide* is one of the most successful series of nature guides ever published in the United States. The Peterson Field Guide series utilized Peterson's unique method of grouping similar species together on the same page and using arrows to designate important field marks, a method for identifying birds now known as the Peterson Identification System. Before this system, guidebooks required numerous observations and measurements, which made it difficult to identify live birds. Peterson's ability to create a visual identification system instead of a scientific one proved valuable in other areas of aviation as well: At the request of the US Army Corps of Engineers, the nation's favorite ornithologist helped create a plane-spotting manual during World War II.

Peterson released his second bird guide, *A Field Guide to Western Birds*, in 1941. Due to the enormous popularity of his books, Peterson's publisher decided to expand his identification system to cover other aspects of the natural world. Before long, Peterson's best-selling series was booming; today it consists of more than 50 guides, 14 coloring books, 6 audio recordings, and 2 instructional videos. After the publication of his first few books, Peterson was able to travel the world painting, observing, and recording the most exceptional and obscure birds. Peterson continued to receive recognition throughout his distinguished career. In 1944, the American Ornithologists' Union presented Peterson with its highest honor, the William Brewster Memorial Award. In 1950, he received the John Burroughs Medal for commendable nature writing. He was given over 20 honorary doctorates and twice nominated for the Nobel Peace Prize; in 1980 President Carter presented him with the Presidential Medal of Freedom.

Roger Tory Peterson passed away on July 28, 1996. In his 87 years, he enhanced the lives of millions of people through his teachings and love of nature. Many believe he did more to encourage public interest in the natural world than any other American of his time.

THE THOUGHT BROUGHT ME UP SHORT. *"You don't suppose she meant the field on the other side of the house?"*

It didn't seem likely. Linda's instructions had been simple and direct: the bird is in the field across the street from the house with the blue whale in the back yard (which really narrows down the options). And we *had* searched that field, not twenty minutes ago, turning up one Eastern Kingbird, two species of swallow—but no Fork-tailed Flycatcher.

But, "across the street from the house with the blue whale" is not

FROM TALES OF A
LOW-RENT BIRDER
BY PETE DUNNE

as interpretation-free as you might think. I'm a product of suburbia, born and raised in one of the planned labyrinths that popped up in the post-war era. *Across the street* to the suburbanized mind invariably means: across the street from the *front* of the house (which is the only across the street a suburban kid ever knows). There are next-door neighbors, back-yard neighbors, but only one *across-the-street neighbor*.

Farm houses, of course, are different, particularly farm houses that sit on corners—like this one did. A farm house that sits on a corner has, potentially, two fields that might be construed to be "across the street."

But, I still didn't give this alternate street theory much credence. The bird, quite simply, had disappeared overnight. A Fork-tailed Flycatcher hadn't lingered in Cape May since Otway Brown had run into this tine-tailed tropical waif back in 1939. It was gone.

But being only one member of a five-member team didn't give me the right to leap to any unilateral decisions. I felt duty-bound to throw the possibility out to the floor.

"You know," I said, "we didn't check the field *next* to the house with the blue whale."

Everybody stopped. Nobody said a word.

"It's probably not worth going back for," I added. "We're thirty minutes behind schedule as it is."

"Oh, come on," Pete Bacinski lobbied. "It's not *that* far out of the way."

"We could just go up Bayshore Road on the way out," Bill Boyle suggested. "Just a quick stop."

"I think it's worth trying," David Sibley added.

I turned to meet the gaze of the fifth member of our Big Day birding team, a man whose face would be recognized instantly in any

FROM TALES OF A LOW-RENT BIRDER

birding spot in North America—a man whom I have known nearly all my life but met for the first time barely twenty-four hours ago.

"Yes, let's give it a try," said Roger Tory Peterson.

All my life doesn't seem like a very long time, now, but it would have seemed interminably long to the scrawny kid who used to wait anxiously next to the mail box on Roosevelt Avenue in Whippany, New Jersey. No zip code. They didn't have zip codes back then.

He was waiting for the red, white, and blue mail truck that was moving down the street, methodically stopping at each yard like a hummingbird going down a row of flowers. He was waiting for the manila envelope with the bold blue label that read—FROM NATIONAL AUDUBON SOCIETY: FOR PETER J. DUNNE. Inside were leaflets, Junior Audubon Society leaflets all about different birds. They were ten cents each—if you ordered six, they were only five cents each. But even five cents each was tough on a budget of thirty-five cents a month and it had taken a long time to get all the leaflets he had wanted.

He had gotten the one about the Baltimore Oriole (State Bird of Maryland), Leaflet No. 26, first along with the Red-winged Blackbird (Leaflet No. 25) because it was common in the tussock-grass marshes near his parents' house (and because it was one of the first birds he had identified). He had added Barn Swallow (Leaflet No. 32), Yellow

Warbler (No. 139), and Indigo Bunting (No. 27). He'd never seen an Indigo Bunting (the bird was simply too beautiful to ever see), but he had gotten the leaflet anyway—just in case.

Each leaflet contained a color plate (that he called a picture) and a matching line drawing (to color in). And he read those leaflets, and read them and read them—until there wasn't any need to anymore, because he had memorized them. They were written by a man named Roger T. Peterson.

When the boy was twelve, he received a marvelous gift—a two-volume book about birds published by the National Geographic Society. Inside the book about *Song and Garden Birds* was an essay by Roger Peterson entitled "What Bird is That?" It described the Peterson System for identifying birds. There were eight questions to ask when you wanted to identify a bird—and the boy memorized them, too.

These were the books he used as his field guides. They used lots of photos. So, it's not surprising that for several years Hermit Warblers were regular spring migrants through Whippany and waterthrushes went unidentified. New Jersey wasn't exactly what you would call "Northern" but it was *still* a long way from Louisiana. He didn't know any other birders so he didn't find out about *real* field guides until

some years later (in fact, until after he'd worked the waterthrush problem out). And, know what? The field guide was written by his old friend and mentor, Roger Peterson.

But even that is a long time ago, now; a distant point on a road that carried a suburban kid with an interest in birds to Cape May, New Jersey. And all along the route, there was a man named Peterson. A man who had helped and guided millions of young minds (just like his). The man who taught first one generation, then another, and another the skills they needed to learn about and enjoy the world they found around them—Roger Tory Peterson.

These were some of the thoughts that skittered across my mind one day last January when I called Dr. Peterson at his home. An idea was developing, an exciting idea. We were thinking about modifying the big day birding tradition and birdathon concept to incorporate an element of competition—*team* competition. On May 19, 1984, big day birding teams representing birding clubs and organizations from several states would bird New Jersey, using all of their knowledge and skills to locate as many birds as possible. There was much to commend the idea. But, there were uncertainties, too. And it would be unthinkable to contemplate an event that would carry birding onto uncharted ground without soliciting the wisdom of the Grand Master of North American Birding. How would he regard the idea? Would he favor it? I needn't have worried.

"It's the next logical step," he said with a conviction that would have put even the most doubtful mind at ease. "Did you know," he continued, "that the British have been holding a two-team competition for several years, now. I've just written an introduction to a book about it called *The Big Bird Race*," he continued, infectiously enthusiastic. "I'll send you a copy. You'll probably want to read it..."

And then he said something that sent my mind tumbling end over end.

"Whose team can I be on? Can I be on yours? We should start at Troy Meadows, don't you think? And then move on toward Boonton for passerines at dawn..."

This, in case you are not a birder, is a little like having the Pope ask whether he can go to church with you on Sunday.

"...*Let's give it a try*," said Roger Tory Peterson, the man with the fine spun frosting of hair that frames two of the bluest, kindest eyes ever to regard the world. And he said it with good reason.

For one thing, our tally stood at 183 with only two hours of daylight left. There were only eighteen species of birds that we felt that we

still had a shot at gathering between now and midnight. Several of these could be counted on to fail. It was going to take a little luck and a couple of unexpected sightings if we were going to reach our goal of two hundred species in twenty-four hours. We were *so* close—and Fork-tailed Flycatcher was *not* accounted in those eighteen possible species.

But there was another reason. A Fork-tailed Flycatcher is not just your run-of-the-mill unexpected sighting—not even by Cape May standards. It would, in fact, be a North American life bird for four of our party. Yes, including Roger—Number 697.

The Fork-tailed story had started twenty-four hours earlier when a couple had walked into Cape May Bird Observatory and confronted Mary Gustafson and Linda Mills with a story about a bird with a short, forked tail that was either some sort of tern—or "possibly a Fork-tailed Flycatcher." The bird was chasing insects in a plowed field.

Thirty minutes later, Linda was back at CMBO, pouring details into the phone. I was on the other end, in a familiar kitchen in Whippany, New Jersey, offering congratulations and fending off mild attacks of disappointment. A malfunctioning radio had cost me a Fork-tailed Flycatcher in 1978; now, fate, it seemed, had taken another. Linda and Mary were going to call all of the local members of the Cape May birding block (those that stood a chance of getting to Cape May Point before dark) but neither knew how to change the hotline carrying five minutes of information crucial to the thirteen teams competing in the first annual World Series of Birding. Besides, Fork-tailed Flycatchers *never* linger. The bird would be gone for sure on Saturday.

For my part, I didn't give the bird another thought until the members of the Guerrilla Birding Team—Bacinski, Boyle, Peterson, Sibley, and I—met in the lobby of the Old Mill Inn in Bernardsville for one last-minute briefing. One hour later, we were on the old dike road that cuts across the Great Swamp, listening in a cold, penetrating drizzle for a Virginia Rail that never called.

Somewhere under the cover of darkness, twelve other teams of birders were moving like clouds on a moonless night. They were testing their abilities, not because they doubted them, but because our species seems driven to reach for what is just out of reach. What was out of reach was two hundred species of birds in a single day. No birder and no group of birders had ever recorded two hundred or more species, under the sun or moon, in New Jersey—or for that matter in any state except California, Texas, and Alabama.

52

FROM TALES OF A LOW-RENT BIRDER

There are those who snort, stamp their feet, and mutter indignantly about the simplemindedness that makes grown people want to stand in the rain at midnight or crisscross a state, ringing up birds with the abandon of kids at the Easter egg hunt on the White House lawn. "It's not bird-watching," they scream righteously. "It's foolishness." And so it is!

But tomorrow, those same birders who were focusing all of the skills accrued during a lifetime of study onto the location of birds by sight and sound would be standing in the South Cape May meadows, watching the antics of feeding shorebirds or wrapped in a warbler fallout at Higbee Beach—and loving it. The very same ones!

One of the most compelling things about this activity called *birding* is the breadth of its scope. It can accommodate both the hard-core lister and the backyard feeder birder. In fact, it is so generous in its scope that it can, at once, accommodate not only big day birders, but even people who object to them!

Isn't birding wonderful.

Our route carried us to the Black River (for more birds that make noises in the dark) and then to the elevated railroad bed at Waterloo, New Jersey. It was a cold dawn, a gray dawn. The air hung damp and

53

still. Cinders crunched underfoot as we drew abreast of the field flanked by tight formations of hedges. Quickly we formed a line, facing the field with a bloodless dawn at our backs. It was not a hopeful morning for birds.

But this was no ordinary commander marshalling our effort. It was North American Birding Himself who was standing on the roadbed that morning, feet comfortably spaced, head turned slightly askew, his features tense, waiting. And we stood in his shadow, mere knights and rooks in the presence of the Master and as the dawn broadened behind us, we watched his mastery unfold.

"Blue-winged Warbler," he said, jabbing the air with his finger for emphasis and guidance. "Field Sparrow . . . Brown Thrasher . . . catbird . . . Canada Warbler . . . Northern Waterthrush . . . White-throated Sparrow. . . ."

"I missed it," a voice said matter-of-factly.

"There," said Roger.

"Got it," the same voice replied.

"Flicker . . . Chipping Sparrow . . . Yellow-throat . . . Chestnut-sided Warbler. . . ."

"Missed it," another voice said, momentarily stopping the flow.

54

"Where?"

"Behind us," said Roger. "Alternate song," someone else suggested helpfully.

It called again. "Got it."

And these were no ordinary lieutenants flanking the Master, not the Bacinskis and Boyles and Sibleys of this world. One by one, each crucial songster was grabbed by the ears—a distant Worm-eating Warbler, a flyover Purple Finch, a lingering Solitary Vireo (making an off, three-note call)—each bird a small victory, one step closer to two hundred species.

At Princeton's Institute Woods, we were ambushed by a fanatical band of Peterson admirers brandishing a formidable arsenal of unsigned field guides. We barely escaped with our civility intact. At Brigantine National Wildlife Refuge, a CBS camera crew mounted a fifth-column movement—assisted by members of a rival team who intimated to fellow birders that "you-know-who is in the car behind you—but don't tell anyone we told you."

There were great victories along our route—Orange-crowned Warbler . . . Ruddy Duck; and bitter defeats—*No* Summer Tanager! *No* kingfisher! *No* Broad-winged Hawk!!! And, here, now, at the very tip

55

of New Jersey, with our total at 183 species, there was just the slimmest measure of hope that the goal of two hundred species was within our reach. And maybe, just maybe, a Fork-tailed Flycatcher.

We began our retreat through the meadows, according to our fatigue. Quickly we loaded the scopes in the car. Four doors slammed shut with the smartness of a parade-ground salute. The Mercedes moved out of the lot for the short drive up Bayshore Road—our second time up that road today.

The car drew slowly to a stop, midway down the length of a plowed field. The blue whale grinned widely off to our left. Indifferently, I brought my binoculars up and felt the others imitate the gesture. Several kingbirds perched casually on a row of bushes about one hundred yards out—along with a slimmer, longer bird that seemed to have a pale, blue back: Fork-tailed Flycatcher.

"There it is," David said.

"I got it," I said, unable to keep the surprise out of my voice.

The car emptied *immediately*. Five scopes emerged from the trunk amid a frenzy of arms and tripods. At 22x the bird stood out like a Peterson plate: a young bird, lacking the long streamer tail feathers of

an adult. Under scrutiny, it made a short sortie into the field, grabbed something, and moved back to take its perch.

"I haven't got it yet," Pete said in tones that barely disguised his anxiety.

"On the ground," I said. "Here, it's in the scope."

David's silence and studied expression left nothing to question. Bill's fine focusing maneuvers at the helm of his Questar overshadowed any doubts from that quarter.

Roger?

His scope stopped moving. His hand touched the focus wheel lightly, and North America's birding patriarch gave his attention to the eyepiece—and whatever lay beyond.

"Yes," he said quietly, intently. "Yes," he said, straightening up, smiling widely. "I've seen the bird, you know, in Mexico. But it is my first for North America."

We knew.

We gave the bird two minutes of study—two minutes more than we had to spare, and left, heading north. There was less than two hours of daylight left. And sixteen species to go.

57

In order to see birds, it is necessary
to become part of the silence.

Roger Tory Peterson

A FEW FEATHERED FACTOIDS

You may know everything there is to know about birdcalls and the migrational patterns of swallows, but what about that great party trivia? Here are a few fun facts to keep even non-birders interested through the wine-and-cheese hour.

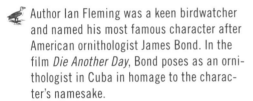 Author Ian Fleming was a keen birdwatcher and named his most famous character after American ornithologist James Bond. In the film *Die Another Day*, Bond poses as an orni- thologist in Cuba in homage to the charac- ter's namesake.

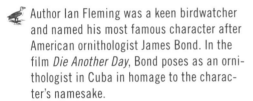 The Whistling Swan has 25,216 feathers on its body, the most of any bird.

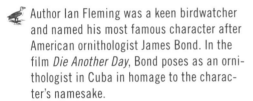 A homing pigeon known as Cher Ami lost an eye and a leg while carrying a message in World War I. Cher Ami won the French Croix de Guerre for his heroic service in delivering 12 important messages, once saving more than 200 American soldiers. Even after being shot, he continued flying until he made it to his destination. His leg was eventually replaced with a wooden one, and he returned to the United States as a war hero.

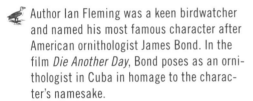 An Australian Pelican's bill measures the longest of all birds at 18.5 inches.

The American Turkey Vulture helps human engineers detect cracked or broken underground natural gas pipes. The smell of the ethyl mercaptan present in the gas attracts the Turkey Vultures due to their keen sense of smell—the clustered birds show repair people where the lines need fixing.

A wryneck's tongue is two-thirds of its body length (excluding the tail).

So you think your mother-in-law talks too much? Try putting her in a room with the famed African Gray Parrot, which boasts an astonishing vocabulary of 800 words, and see who out-talks whom.

There is a group of African Social Weavers that reside in a 100-chamber nest structure that's 27 feet in length and 6 feet high.

In 1850, Paul Reuter, who later founded Reuters press agency, used a fleet of more than 45 pigeons to transmit news and stock price updates between Brussels and Aachen.

Many states share the same official state bird, with the Cardinal representing the most—seven!

Nightingales can have as many as 300 different love songs in their repertoires.

Canaries may take 30 mini breaths a second to replenish their air supply.

Cowbirds use 40 different notes in their songs, some so high that humans are unable to hear them.

A group of crows in Japan have figured out an ingenious way to crack walnuts for meals—they drop them on the road and wait for cars to drive over them.

The Clark's Nutcracker, a type of North American crow, collects up to 30,000 pine seeds over three weeks in November and buries them across an area of 200 square miles. Over the next eight months, it succeeds in retrieving more than 90 percent of the seeds, even those covered in feet of snow.

Japanese White-naped Cranes, which migrate between Japan and China, happily use the tension-filled three-quarter-mile-wide Demilitarized Zone between North and South Korea as a stopover site to replenish their reserves for the second leg of their migration.

Camouflage is key for some birds. The winter plumage of the Willow Ptarmigan is white to help it blend in with its snowy winter home, but its spring molt produces mottled brown feathers, making the female almost invisible as she sits on her nest.

The Winter Wren sings such a long song—seemingly minutes on end, then repeated over and over—that the Ojibwa named this bird *Ka-wa-miti-go-shi-que-na-go-mooch*.

Basic Bird Identification

YOU ARE OUT WORKING in your garden when a little brown bird catches your eye, and like any good beginning birder you wonder to yourself what species it is. But while you are running into the shed for your field guide, the bird is off to another yard and you've lost it. Knowing the basics of identification can help you enjoy the bird now and look it up later.

Bird identification is as simple as asking yourself the right questions to narrow down what you might be seeing. Using the process of elimination, these questions will allow you to zoom in on various qualities of the bird that will help you identify it. And being able to properly identify a bird means that when you tell your family at dinner there was a bird in your feeder, you can state confidently whether it was a Black-capped Chickadee or a White-breasted Nuthatch. Which sounds much more impressive than saying, "*Some LBJ*", don't you think?

Let's go back to your garden. When you see the mystery bird, first ask yourself: How big is it? Remember, **size** can be difficult to determine because of the distance between you and the bird. Distance can make even the largest birds look miniature, and misjudging size will definitely throw you off track. If you aren't sure you're making an accurate assessment, try comparing it with an object. If a bird is perched on a gardening tool, for example, is it wider or smaller than the tool? You can always go back and measure the object after the bird has left. Determining the size of birds in flight can also be tough. Usually larger birds fly in wider circles than smaller ones, and their flight tends to be more intentional and less uninhibited or acrobatic. The wings of larger birds also beat at a slower pace.

Once you have determined size, it's helpful to establish the **shape**. Make a few observations: What is the length of the tail? Is the bird's build thin or stocky? Is the bill narrow and pointed or thick and downturned? At times, beak shape alone can help tell you what type of bird it is, as birds are grouped for identification mostly by structural similarities.

Next, zoom in on other key visual clues—**field marks** or distinguishing patterns. These marks include lines above the eye, eye rings, stripes on the crown, patches on the wings, spots on the tail, and bibs of various colors on the chest. Be careful when noting field marks: Some are visible only when the bird is in flight, hidden beneath the wings.

Over time and with practice you will also learn to recognize bird **behavior**, a tool that can make the identification process much easier. You may be able to recognize a bird just by how it sits or stands, and knowing what a bird likes to eat or its movements will also help you distinguish it from other birds that otherwise look strikingly similar.

To recap: size, shape (of body and bill), field marks, and behavior. Knowing all these details can help you when you're ready to head to your field guide after you've fully enjoyed observing your new bird friend.

A Few More Helpful Tips

- Purchase a CD of local birdcalls to get acquainted with their songs. Soon you will be identifying birds before you even see them!
- Study your field guide when not birdwatching. Knowing basic

facts about birds habitats and migration patterns can help you narrow down your choices to those species you can expect to see in your area.

- Keeping checklists of certain variables will help to eliminate other birds from your list of possibilities. Some birds (owls, for instance) come out only at certain times; noting the time and location of your sighting will help you draw conclusions. Often checklists are available at popular birding locations.

- Sketch what you are seeing. This will help you take notice of obvious traits like size, color, field marks, and other important characteristics.

W. ~~ars sc.

IN THE LIST OF DEBTS to those who shaped my first years of
birding the oldest of my IOUs is made out to my brother Andy.
One Christmas he received a cheap pair of Boots 8x30 binoculars.
I'm not sure why he wanted some, but when I took up birds he
generously allowed me to use them. I have to confess that I didn't
so much borrow as commandeer them. And once I'd started to go
to Lightwood or on the Buxtom Field Club outings he never really
saw them again. By the time I replaced them I actually thought they
were mine.

Not that they
were any good.
In fact they were
useless. Had I used
them for much
longer I'd probably

FROM B I R D E R S :
TALES OF A TRIBE
BY MARK COCKER

have suffered permanent eye damage. But *then* I thought they were
wonderful and I still remember them clearly and with affection—
the chipped black-metal body, the star-burst flaws in the object
lenses, the staples that held the leather straps together.

They were the first object of desire in a long relationship
with optical technology; an affair that's central to most birders'
lives and which borders on a marriage. Currently mine is a neatly

69

bigamous arrangement—the second pair is kept permanently on the desk, while a pair of Leica 8x32s, my first consort as it were, accompanies me wherever I go.

But compared with other birders this promiscuity is modest. Many have the equivalent of an optical harem: pairs for the car, for work, a pair downstairs and maybe one in the bedroom, a little pocketable set for non-birding situations, and several others just in case. Steve Gantlett and Richard Millington, joint editors of *Birding World*, with homes overlooking the legendary reserve at Cley in Norfolk, have telescopes and tripods permanently in place on the landing.

It goes without saying that when you're out birding, you have a pair of binoculars around your neck all day. When you go into a shop or sit down for a drink, or a meal, you'd never dream of taking them off. This physical attachment is more than simply a case of being prepared for the unexpected. Birders sometimes keep them on when they go to conferences or society meetings, or any function where the main focus is birds. Occasionally they actually use them. At slide talks it feels much more like the real thing to line up at the back of the hall, watching the bird images on screen through a pair of 8x40s.

FROM BIRDERS: TALES OF A TRIBE

Even more strange, though, is the fact that birders take their binoculars to the Rutland Bird Fair. This is an annual event held over three days and represents the biggest bird jamboree in the world. It takes place at the nature reserve of Rutland Water, but seeing birds is not a high priority. It's a moment when everyone involved in the industry (and I use that word deliberately)—clubs, societies, bird-book sellers, wildlife-holiday companies and, especially, manufacturers of optics—gathers to tout their wares. The exhibitors are there for commercial and possibly social purposes, while the thousands of punters wander through half a dozen huge marquees sampling the fare on several hundred stands. And many do this with the best part of a thousand pounds' worth of optics around their necks. Often they even have a telescope and tripod dangling at their side for good measure.

It looks strange, but it's only inexplicable if the bins and scope (no one really talks about binoculars or telescopes) are presumed to have a practical function. Their true purpose is a statement about identity. It's this, what you might call the psychology of optics, which fascinates me.

FROM BIRDERS: TALES OF A TRIBE

First we need to consider a few technical details. From their origins in the nineteenth century binoculars have followed the same basic format. They are, in essence, a pair of metal tubes with openings at either end for the light to enter and exit. The larger end, the far end, is known as the objective or object lens and is the part that receives the light from the subject being viewed. The light rays then travel through the tube, bouncing off a sequence of glass prisms before exiting at the ocular, or eyepiece, having been magnified by internal lenses in the process...

While the principles determining which bins to use have largely remained the same, the quality of the optics has changed out of all recognition. Most of the earlier manufacturers were probably producing them for military or naval purposes and you could tell. They seemed to work on a standard axiom that fighting men needed equipment that measured up to their machismo and if the bins didn't hang around your neck like lead weights they couldn't possibly be decent lenses. Many were shaped like two huge barrels each the length of a small lighthouse. They'd have specifications like 16x60.

Often they had no central focusing mechanism and each eyepiece had to be adjusted independently. I could imagine them

in the hands of someone watching the horizon for an enemy aircraft carrier. Or possibly someone scanning from the crow's nest of a whaling vessel. But you could tell they hadn't been designed for spotting leaf warblers flitting through the treetops. Sometimes the image produced was bisected by a pair of hair-line sights, or even a grid of intersecting lines with numbers down the side. Looking through them, you felt you were not so much intended to identify birds as blow them up.

But when I first started—dare I call it the old days?—ancient binoculars carried no stigma. In fact, many people thought old was good. To look weather-beaten, to have a pound of grit on the inside of your object lens, and to have them worn down to pure brass on those parts that were in contact with the body—these were paraded like old battle scars. Like 'my' old Boots 8x30s, these sorts of bins were completely useless, but their perversely loyal owners would hand them to you for examination, boasting they'd recently compared them with a new top model, and there hadn't been much in it. Admittedly most other people did have a few problems focusing. But what did you think?

Then you'd look down and find a dim monochrome scene swimming out of focus behind a fog of scratchmarks, black specks

and what looked like green fungus growing on the prisms. You'd hand them back feeling slightly queasy, with some polite comment about them possibly needing a bit of a service.

But if, in the old days, the bins were bad, the scopes were even worse. In the early 1970s most people relied solely on their bins, but if they were serious then they had to make a choice between one of only three new telescope models, the Nickel Supra, the Hertel and Reuss and the Swift Telemaster. The Nickel was dreadful. It was like looking down the cardboard tube from a toilet roll. The Hertel, the scope I eventually bought, was much better. It was like looking through the cardboard tube from a kitchen roll. Like the Nickel, the Hertel was a zoom scope, and you could twist the lens out to increase magnification from twenty-five to sixty times. I used to love sitting in a hide and watching waders at minimum distance with maximum magnification, so that you could see every detail on, say, a Snipe's tertials. You were so close to the beast you felt you knew what it was like to be a feather louse.

I have to confess that optically the best of the three scope options was the Swift Telemaster. The only disadvantage with it was it was so short. In those days you didn't have a tripod to stand it on, as everyone does today. Birders had to either find something

74

to rest it on, usually a friend's shoulder or a fence post; otherwise you had to adopt the standard birder-using-scope position, which was lying on your back, legs crossed with the telescope's object lens balanced on the side of your calf and your spine tilted upwards so you could get your eye to the other end. Unfortunately the Swift Telemaster was so short that that position was a physical impossibility. It's probably why most people either had a Nickel or a Hertel, for all their shortcomings. But even with one of these two, using it while on your back was like achieving one of the postures in Iyengar yoga. Some birders blame a lifetime of back trouble on adopting that position.

There was one way to alleviate the problem and that was to obtain an old brass telescope—the sort that you see ghillies using in ancient photos of people deer-stalking. If you can't imagine one of these, think of Nelson holding a scope to his unseeing eye, then multiply its length by three. The old brass scopes were huge and their original manufacture was probably also for military purposes, but up until the 1970s a brass scope was also a key insignia of a *real* birder. I always lamented that I never had one.

They were difficult to find and not easy to use when you did. A key problem was their weight. When not extended the brass

75

sections concertina-ed together and were snugly housed in leather sockets that were permanently attached to the strap. Unfortunately that solid cylinder of metal weighed a ton. Birders carrying them tended to lean with one scope-burdened shoulder slightly lower than the other. But brass scopes really came into their own when you were lying down, since it was relatively straightforward to rest a three-foot-long pipe on your leg and look out the other end. However, as the birder and TV comedian Bill Oddie made clear in a wonderful description of his own scope, holding that position for any length of time was no mean feat. 'Can you conceive how excruciatingly agonising that was?' Oddie recalls:

If not, you might care to try it sometime. If you can't find an old brass scope, a large cucumber will do. And, come to think of it, it will probably be about as effective optically. And don't just do it for a few minutes; stay there for several hours. Then try and get up. I promise you, you'll have a new-found respect for the legendary old seawatchers who used to lie there for days looking at nothing off Selsey Bill. Then again, you might realise that they weren't so much dedicated as stuck. People died in that position and no one realised for months. If you did survive you were left with a posture like the Hunchback of Notre Dame. But we wore our stoop with pride.

FROM BIRDERS: TALES OF A TRIBE

The great advantage of these scopes, which Bill Oddie doesn't mention, was their sheer ruggedness. For instance, it could double up as a fantastic weapon. Birders can get into pretty lonely, potentially hazardous, situations. But most people would think twice about taking on someone wielding a three-foot tube of brass. And then there was always the opportunity for do-it-yourself entertainment. There is a wonderful old story of birders on the Isles of Scilly who, when the birds were thin on the ground, had a scope-throwing competition, a birder's equivalent of tossing the caber. The great thing about brass scopes was that there was no loss of quality through such handling. They were always crap.

Massive improvements in optical technology during the last twenty years have had a revolutionising effect on birding... But they've also done away with some of the old social certainties. A problem that's become more acute is that of identifying the abilities of a birding stranger. There was a time when you could assume that someone possessing good binoculars automatically knew what they were talking about, which was critical when you wanted to know what birds were around. A serious birder, even if he were the most impoverished teenager, would strive to own a pair of

Zeiss or Leitz, the two top brands until the 1980s. In fact the depth of contrast between the optics' value and the impoverished appearance of their owner was the best index of ability. Spot a young guy in raggedy old T-shirt, baseball boots, jeans that hadn't been washed for weeks, *plus* a pristine pair of Zeiss 10x40s, and you were clearly on safe ground. It told you that most of that birder's entire worldly wealth was round his neck. Today, unfortunately, expensive binoculars indicate almost nothing. Birding has entered the mainstream of consumer culture. Today you can meet a couple decked out with £3000 worth of optics and it will tell you little of sociological importance, except the ludicrous follies of conspicuous consumption.

But one thing the new range of super-bins has done is intensify further the key experience which *all* optical equipment, however bad, confers on its user—those sensations of liberty and clarity that are so much more difficult to find in ordinary life. If you can't imagine what I'm talking about, then try it. Worried about your job, your relationship, money, sex or how you're going to pay for the £1000 pair of binoculars you've just bought on credit? Then raise them to your eyes, look at those five gulls beating a

78

determined path across the sky, or that small murmuration of starlings swirling above the city, and the problem's on its way to being solved. Or at least it's nowhere to be seen.

Most binoculars allow you about eight degrees of vision. It means that for the moments you hold them to your eyes, the other 352 degrees are completely excluded. Anything within the orbit of those eight degrees is magnified and enhanced, while everything else—job, relationship, money, sex—is consigned to the aura of darkness around you. That, in a nutshell is the joy, the magic, of binoculars. They convert life into something else, something almost abstract, something purer, clearer, usually more beautiful and almost always something you'd never really seen that way before. That's what birders are hooked on—not the physical object, the complex prisms and lenses of binoculars, but their wondrous alchemical power to transform you and your state of being. When I saw those Meadow Pipits grovelling around in fields at Lightwood, or that Short-eared Owl sailing above the moors at Goldsitch Moss it was this new way of seeing, as much as the birds themselves, which transfixed me. And life could never be the same again.

Beginning Binocs

THE SINGLE MOST IMPORTANT tool for any beginning birder is that first pair of binoculars. Finding the perfect pair, and learning the correct way to use them, is a great first step on the path to becoming a happy birder.

When shopping for your binoculars (or your *binocs*, *bins*, or *optics*, as they're called in the trade), comfort is the first and foremost factor to consider. Prices can vary—we'll get to that—but aren't reflective of comfort level. Every face is unique, so the key to finding comfortable binoculars is taking them for a test run in the store. Ask yourself: Is it difficult to raise them to my eyes? Does my forefinger rest easily on the focus wheel? Am I able to adjust the lenses to the right width for my face? Is their weight around my neck going to slow me down?

Remember that when you're out in the field, in the garden, or sitting by your kitchen window, you want your binoculars to be your eyes, not a pain in your neck.

Once you've found the perfect fit, take a peek at the price tag. If you're in shock, keep in mind that you should expect to spend at least $100 for binoculars that have high-quality glass and are durable enough to last you a lifetime.

There are two basic types of bins. **Porro-prism** binoculars are the classic, wide-bodied shape that will be familiar if you ever borrowed the pair Grandpa kept in the attic. Designed in the mid-1800s, porros are still a great choice. The lenses let in light and have very little light reflection, which can cause image distortion. On the downside, these binocs can be heavy, and their bulk can make them difficult for younger birders.

Roof-prism binoculars are the sleeker, lighter alternative.

These offer slightly higher magnification for faraway objects, but they do tend to be more expensive and don't focus as closely, making it difficult to focus on those birds that land—miraculously—just under your nose.

Once you find the perfect bins to fit your needs, a few tips will help you use them correctly. Many new birders grow frustrated right away when they're unable to locate through their binoculars the bird they've just spotted with the naked eye. Indeed, in the scramble to get your optics up to your face, pointed in the right direction, focused, and steadied, you may not immediately see the branch that a gorgeous Yellow Warbler just perched on. Relax. Once you've spotted him with your naked eye, lock your eyes on him and don't move—simply bring the binoculars up to your face without changing the level of your gaze. Voilà, you've just achieved an unbelievable proximity to your new warbling friend.

83

O<small>THER TIPS FROM THE PROS</small>:

- Always carry your binoculars around your neck with a supportive neck strap.
- Never look directly at the sun.
- Keep your lenses spotless with the lens-cleaning supplies available from your local camera store.
- If you're feeling dizzy, clean your lenses or take your binocs in for readjustment.
- If you're getting "warbler neck" from too many hours of staring straight up into the sky, give yourself a rest by stretching out flat on the ground and doing your birding from there!

BINOCULAR ACCESSORIES

By Ben, Cathryn, and John Sill

Binoculars are still the single most important item for the successful birder. Most of the "binocs" on the market today are similarly constructed—black, two barrels, lens covers, a focusing mechanism, strap, and a carrying case. With a little study, it will become obvious that adherence to TRADITION has stunted binocular advancement. Galileo would feel as much at home with twentieth-century binoculars as he did with those developed shortly after his death. In an effort to move ahead, the following items are reviewed for the serious birder.

BIFOCAL BINOCULARS

When you reach that awkward age when you can't see well up close with your glasses and can't see at distances without them (or the other way around), most people opt for bifocals. Now, a little-known company in the Midwest has developed a set of bifocal binoculars. This allows you to focus on birds which are so close that you don't even need the binoculars. When properly fitted, you can even read your field guide through the binoculars, thus saving time. This company also offers numerous other combinations such as:

- Bifocal Monoculars

- Trifocal Binoculars

- Bifocal Trinoculars

- Monofocal Binoculars

- Bimono Focaloculars

FLIP DOWNS

Have you ever been watching a swallow dart and dive as it streaks across the sky, only to have it pass in front of the sun, accompanied by your comment of "ARRRGHHH!!!!!"? With new Flip Down sunglass binoculars, you can avoid this problem. They are manufactured by the same reputable company that makes a similar product for major league baseball.

BINOCULAR BIRD WHEEL

Often, when you see a new bird, it will fly just as you put your binoculars down and are thumbing frantically through a field guide. The Bird Wheel solves this problem once and for all. By attaching it to the end of your binoculars, you can rotate a series of bird silhouettes in front of each lens while still looking at the bird. Just keep rotating until the silhouette matches that of the bird. Shore birds and hawks are on the left wheel, and perching birds are on the right wheel. Other wheels are available if desired. For example, farmers can purchase chickens on the left wheel, and turkeys on the right.

SEMI-AUTOMATIC FOCUSSING BINOCULARS

This new accessory helps the novice to rapidly and accurately focus on a bird. It comes with an ergonomically molded, two-pound brass weight (won't rust), attached to a strong 100-yard long monofilament line, marked off in 2-foot increments. Metric markings are also available on request. After locating a bird, all you do is toss the weight to the bird's location, read off the distance on the line, and then focus your binoculars to that distance. With practice, it is seldom necessary to throw the weight more than two or three times. Comes with a special spool for rewinding the line. While effective for single birds, things get a bit frantic when used for flocks. Doesn't work too well for birds in flight, or for sea birds.

Assateague Island off the shores of Virginia is known as the home of more than 300 wild ponies, but it also hosts over 300 resident and migrating bird species. Take a birdwatching boat tour along the protected inner coastal waters to see Black Skimmers, Oystercatchers, Bald Eagles, and Ospreys.

Located along the Tennessee River in Alabama, Wheeler National Wildlife Refuge offers extraordinary numbers

Birding in the South

of shorebirds and wading birds for visitors during the winter months, as well as one of the southernmost concentrations of Canada Geese. It's also the winter habitat of the largest duck population in the state!

For a glimpse at endangered birds, look no farther than Florida's Everglades National Park. Along with the endangered Wood Stork and Snail Kite, lucky visitors might see Swallow-tailed Kites, Mottled Ducks, and Purple Gallinules.

If Roseate Spoonbills are more your style, check out J. N. Ding Darling

National Wildlife Refuge on Sanibel Island, where you can find a good percentage of the US population of these avians at any time. Stay for a whole day as the bird population shifts with the tide and you might check off the American Bittern, White Ibis, Tricolored Heron, and Pileated Woodpecker on your life list!

Spring is a great time to be at Okefenokee National Wildlife Refuge, where you can catch the courtship dance of the Sandhill Crane in March and see baby cranes hatch as alligators mate and insect-eating pitcher plants bloom in April. All year long, you can also see the fascinating Anhinga, which uses its long bill to spear frogs and water snakes.

Whether you are looking for real birds or just paintings of birds, stop by the John James Audubon State Park in Kentucky. Aside from more than 200 species of birds (including the beloved Rose-breasted Grosbeaks), the park houses the world's largest collection of paintings and memorabilia from Audubon himself.

The world's longest system of caves is in Mammoth Cave National Park,

Kentucky, which tends to attract people who love batwatching. But birdwatchers may want to stay aboveground to see the reintroduced wild turkeys, Kentucky Warblers, and Red-tailed Hawks that are attracted to the area's sandstone.

While in Mississippi, birdwatchers can steal a glimpse of the endangered Red-cockaded Woodpecker at Noxubee National Wildlife Refuge or see one of the largest US populations of Wood Storks at St. Catherine's Creek National Wildlife Reserve.

Swan lovers should plan their trip to North Carolina for the first weekend in December, when Swan Days occurs near Mattamuskeet National Wildlife Refuge. The local town's celebration offers van tours to the refuge featuring places generally off limits to the public.

Huntington Beach State Park in South Carolina showcases the three species of egrets and much more in its saltwater marshes, freshwater lagoons, maritime forest, and beach terrains—all perfect for a day of diverse birdwatching.

Built with waterfowl specifically in mind, Tennessee National Wildlife

Refuge is a major wintering spot for migrating birds. Between December and February, more than 250,000 ducks and 20,000 geese call the reserve home. As a bonus, so do approximately 100 Bald Eagles.

Twelve miles from our nation's capital sits Great Falls Park—a haven for warblers. Of the 50 types found in the continental United States, 34 can be spotted here.

Those southerners who can't make the trip up north for birding should check out West Virginia's Cranesville Swamp Preserve, where the boreal bog attracts rare area birds like the Golden-crowned Kinglet, Northern Saw-whet Owl, and Nashville Warbler.

Winning the 2005 "America's Birdiest Small Coastal City" award is Dauphin Island in Alabama. The entire island is considered a bird sanctuary, and it's a common first stop for birds making the trip north from the Yucatán Peninsula.

If you really want to get away from it all, head to Cape Romain National Wilderness Reserve's Bull Island in South Carolina. The forested barrier of sand is accessible only by a 45-minute boat ride, and the reward for the trip is a wealth of terns, sandpipers, plovers, and pelicans, along with the occasional songbird "fallout."

Swan Lake isn't just a ballet; it's also a national refuge in Missouri where during the fall migration, ducks in the hundreds of thousands stop over. More than 100 Bald Eagles winter here, too.

The largest remaining area of prairie land in Missouri is located in Prairie State Park. There you can find some of the best tallgrass birds, including Dickcissels, Northern Bobwhites, Grasshopper Sparrows, and the Upland Sandpiper.

Another prairie grass habitat in Missouri, the Taberville Prairie Conservation Area, was specifically placed to preserve the habitat of the dwindling Greater Prairie Chicken. When you hear the males' booming call, you know it's time to witness the courtship dance.

Aransas National Wildlife Refuge in Texas is winter home to the only migratory population of the endangered Whooping Crane. Over 200 Whooping Cranes can be seen here on the Gulf Coast between October and March, along with 398 other species of birds.

In Bentsen–Rio Grande Valley State Park and surrounding southern Texas, birders can glimpse more than 30 species not seen anywhere else in the United States, including the Plain Chachalaca and the Green Jay. The Texas park offers reasonable six- to eight-hour birding tours with guides who can help you spot the resident Elf Owls, the smallest owls in the world.

The Flamingos
Jardin des Plantes, Paris
By Rainer Maria Rilke

With all the subtle paints of Fragonard
no more of their red and white could be expressed
than someone would convey about his mistress
by telling you, "She was lovely, lying there

still soft with sleep." They rise above the green
grass and lightly sway on their long pink stems,
side by side, like enormous feathery blossoms,
seducing (more seductively than Phryne)

themselves; till, necks curling, they sink their large
pale eyes into the softness of their down,
where apple-red and jet-black lie concealed.

A shriek of envy shakes the parrot cage;
but *they* stretch out, astonished, and one by one
stride into their imaginary world.

ANY PERSON with no steady job and no children naturally finds the time for a sizable amount of utterly idle speculation. For instance, me—I've developed a theory about crows. It goes like this:

FROM NATURAL ACTS

BY DAVID QUAMMEN

Crows are bored. They suffer from being too intelligent for their station in life. Respectable evolutionary success is simply not, for these brainy and complex birds, enough. They are dissatisfied with the narrow goals and horizons of that tired old Darwinian struggle. On the lookout for a new challenge. See them there, lined up conspiratorially along a fence rail or a high wire, shoulder to shoulder, alert, self-contained, missing nothing. Feeling discreetly thwarted. Waiting, like an ambitious understudy, for their break. Dolphins and whales and chimpanzees get all the fawning publicity, great fuss made over their near-human intelligence. But don't be fooled. Crows are not stupid. Far from it. They are merely underachievers. They are bored.

Most likely it runs in their genes, along with the black plumage and the talent for vocal mimicry. Crows belong to a remarkable family of birds known as the Corvidae, also including ravens, magpies, jackdaws and jays, and the case file on this entire clan is so full of prodigious and quirky behavior that it cries out for interpretation not by an ornithologist but a psychiatrist. Or, failing that, some ignoramus with a supple theory. Computerized ecologists can give us those fancy equations depicting the whole course of a creature's life history in terms of energy allotment to every physical need, with variables for fertility and senility and hunger and motherly love; but they haven't yet programmed in a variable for boredom. No wonder the Corvidae dossier is still packed with unanswered questions.

At first glance, though, all is normal: Crows and their corvid relatives seem to lead an exemplary birdlike existence. The home life is stable and protective. Monogamy is the rule, and most mated pairs stay together until death. Courtship is elaborate, even rather tender, with the male doing a good bit of bowing and dancing and jiving, not to mention supplying his intended with food; eventually he offers the first scrap of nesting material as a sly hint that they get on with it. While she incubates a clutch of four to six eggs, he continues to furnish the groceries, and stands watch nearby at night. Then for a month after hatching, both parents dote on the young. Despite strenuous care, mortality among fledglings is routinely high, sometimes as high as 70 percent, but all this crib death is counterbalanced by the longevity of the adults. Twenty-year-old crows are not unusual, and one raven in captivity survived to age twenty-nine. Anyway, corvids show no inclination toward breeding themselves up to huge numbers, filling the countryside with their kind (like the late passenger pigeon, or an infesting variety of insect) until conditions shift for the worse, and a vast population collapses. Instead, crows and their relatives reproduce at roughly the same stringent rate through periods of bounty or austerity, maintaining levels of population that are modest but consistent, and which can be supported throughout any foreseeable hard times. In this sense they are astute pessimists. One consequence of such modesty of demographic ambition is to leave them with excess time, and energy, not desperately required for survival.

The other thing they possess in excess is brain-power. They have the largest cerebral hemispheres, relative to body size, of any avian family. On various intelligence tests—to measure learning facility, clock-reading skills, the ability to count—they have made other birds look doltish. One British authority, Sylvia Bruce Wilmore, pronounces them "quicker on the uptake" than certain well-thought-of mammals like the cat and the monkey, and admits that her own tamed crow so effectively dominated the other animals in her household that this bird "would even pick up the spaniel's leash and lead him around the garden!" Wilmore also adds cryptically: "Scientists at the University of Mississippi have been successful in getting the cooperation of Crows." But she fails to make clear whether that was as test subjects, or on a consultative basis.

From other crow experts come the same sort of anecdote. Crows hiding food in all manner of unlikely spots and relying on their uncanny memories, like adepts at the game of Concentration, to find the caches again later. Crows using twenty-three distinct forms of call to communicate various sorts of information to each other. Crows in flight dropping clams and walnuts on highway pavement, to break open the shells so the meats can be eaten. Then there's the one about the hooded crow, a species whose range includes Finland: "In this land Hoodies show great initiative during winter when men fish through holes in the ice.

FROM NATURAL ACTS

Fishermen leave baited lines in the water to catch fish and on their return they have found a Hoodie pulling in the line with its bill, and walking away from the hole, then putting down the line and walking back on it to stop it sliding, and pulling it again until [the crow] catches the fish on the end of the line." These birds are bright.

And probably—according to my theory—they are too bright for their own good. You know the pattern. Time on their hands. Under-employed and over-qualified. Large amounts of potential just lying fallow. Peck up a little corn, knock back a few grasshoppers, carry a beak-full of dead rabbit home for the kids, then fly over to sit on a fence rail with eight or ten cronies and watch some poor farmer sweat like a sow at the wheel of his tractor. An easy enough life, but is that *it*? Is this *all*?

If you don't believe me just take my word for it: Crows are bored.

And so there arise, as recorded in the case file, these certain . . . no, *symptoms* is too strong. Call them, rather, *patterns of gratuitous behavior*.

For example, they play a lot.

Animal play is a reasonably common phenomenon, at least

among certain mammals, especially in the young of those species. Play activities—by definition—are any that serve no immediate biological function, and which therefore do not directly improve the animal's prospects for survival and reproduction. The corvids, according to expert testimony, are irrepressibly playful. In fact, they show the most complex play known in birds. Ravens play toss with themselves in the air, dropping and catching again a small twig. They lie on their backs and juggle objects (in one recorded case, a rubber ball) between beak and feet. They jostle each other sociably in a version of "king of the mountain" with no real territorial stakes. Crows are equally frivolous. They play a brand of rugby, wherein one crow picks up a white pebble or a bit of shell and flies from tree to tree, taking a friendly bashing from its buddies until it drops the token. And they have a comedy-acrobatic routine: allowing themselves to tip backward dizzily from a wire perch, holding a loose grip so as to hang upside down, spreading out both wings, then daringly letting go with one foot; finally, switching feet to let go with the other. Such shameless hot-dogging is usually performed for a small audience of other crows.

There is also an element of the practical jokester. Of the Indian house crow, Wilmore says: ". . . this Crow has a sense of

humor, and revels in the discomfort caused by its playful tweaking
at the tails of other birds, and at the ears of sleeping cows and
dogs; it also pecks the toes of flying foxes as they hang sleeping
in their roosts." This crow is a laff riot. Another of Wilmore's
favorite species amuses itself, she says, by "dropping down on
sleeping rabbits and rapping them over the skull or settling on
drowsy cattle and startling them." What we have here is actually
a distinct subcategory of playfulness known, where I come from
at least, as Cruisin' For A Bruisin'. It has been clinically linked
to boredom.

Further evidence: Crows are known to indulge in sunbathing.
"When sunning at fairly high intensity," says another British
corvidist, "the bird usually positions itself sideways on to the sun
and erects its feathers, especially those on head, belly, flanks and
rump." So the truth is out: Under those sleek ebony feathers, they
are tan. And of course sunbathing (like ice-fishing, come to think
of it) constitutes prima facie proof of a state of paralytic ennui....

But maybe it's not too late for the corvids. Keep that in
mind next time you run into a raven, or a magpie, or a crow.
Look the bird in the eye. Consider its frustrations. Try to say
something stimulating.

VERY SUPERSTITIOUS

While you are out birdwatching, keep in mind that you may be seeing not just birds but also omens for your future. Many superstitions surround our feathered friends, but whether you believe in them or not, they are pretty interesting to consider—especially when it concerns possible good fortune for you!

The London Tower keeps a minimum of six Ravens with clipped wings at all times. It is believed that the White Tower will collapse and the monarch will fall if the birds leave. The names of the eight Ravens currently in the tower are Gwylum, Thor, Hugine, Munin, Branwen, Bran, Gundulf, and Baldrick.

Romans thought that the crowing of a cock during a party was a very bad omen indeed. The correct magic spell needed to be cast or nothing could be eaten that day.

Some Romans practiced Augury—the art of divination by observing the behavior of birds. Techniques ranged from taking note of where a bird flew in the sky to interpreting how a group of chickens ate their seeds.

The Irish believe that if you hear a Cuckoo's first spring song, you will find a white hair under your right foot. If you choose to keep this hair on your person, the first name you hear after this will be that of your future wife or husband.

Owls were engraved on the faces of coins in Greece so they could keep a watchful eye on commerce.

A wish made on the first robin of spring will be granted.

To avoid bad luck in England, take your hat off or make the sign of the cross when passing by a magpie.

Sewing the feather of a swan into your husband's pillow will ensure his fidelity.

Never bring a peacock feather inside your home, for it will bring with it bad luck.

Sailors believe that albatross are bearers of good luck. If one is caged or killed, however—even accidentally—it will bring misfortune to the ship and her crew, and death or curse to the sailor who kills it.

A white dove seen flying overhead is considered a good omen.

If you hear a dove while traveling uphill, you will have a year of good luck. Hear one while going downhill, though, and misfortune is headed your way.

A bird tapping at the window is an omen of impending death to one of the house's occupants. This superstition comes from the ancient belief that birds are messengers of departed souls—or even the souls themselves—who have returned to guide those soon to die.

The next time you get hit by bird droppings, don't fret: This is a sign of good things to come.

If a stork builds a nest on your home, you have been blessed and will receive the enduring love of Venus.

Local superstition around Big Bend National Park in Texas says that if you see a roadrunner and it changes directions, you will have bad luck.

A cock crowing at the end of the day signals bad weather to come tomorrow. If it crows all night, as in Shakespeare's *Hamlet*, a death in the family is imminent.

Crows by the numbers: One's bad, two's luck, three's health, four's wealth, five's sickness, six is death.

BIRD CALLS FOR THE ADVANCED BIRDER

By Ben, Cathryn, and John Sill

SPISHING: This is done by loudly whispering the word "spish." You can tell if you are at the proper sound level by placing your hand about a foot in front of your mouth. It should be thoroughly wet after three to five spishes. DO NOT stand too close behind other birders when spishing. This call attracts all those species which happen to respond well to spishing.

SQUEAKING: To do this, pucker up tightly like you are going to kiss someone who you are afraid might suck your lips off. Then draw air in through the tiniest hole that you can make. This should result in a high-pitched squeak. If dogs go berserk or if you attract an inordinate number of bats, then your pucker is a bit too tight.

SNICKERING: This call is effective for birds that respond to a certain kind of unusual noise. First rub your lips with a strong antiperspirant. This will help to keep your lips tight. Next, simply take a 25 cent piece and place it inside your lips, and flat against your closed teeth. Friends should be able to see just the nose of George Washington unless you placed it tails side out. Blow as hard as you can without losing the coin. You should be able to hear clearly the snickering noises of others in your party.

HISSING: Look in the direction of the bird you want to hiss at. Use your forefingers to pull outward at each corner of your mouth and stretch until it hurts. Stick your tongue out of your mouth as far as you can. Exhale forcefully with a hissing sound. This is usually quite effective in provoking activity in both birds and mammals in the vicinity.

WHOOSHING: Hold your breath until you start to turn blue. When you can't stand it any longer, release all your air with a single loud whoosh. Note: repeating frequently until you are light-headed can be a substantial advantage in helping to see new and exotic birds.

PELAGIC CALLS

Birders find calling sea birds quite difficult and often don't attempt it, but I have found that most birders are using the wrong calls. When a seabird is sighted, it is generally from an ocean-going vessel chartered specifically for this purpose. Pelagic trips of this kind often encounter stormy weather and rough seas, and observations indicate that during such conditions, the birds seem drawn to the boat. The reason for this is that the large number of birders leaning over the rails, feeding the fish their own dinners, make a sort of groaning, heaving noise. This seems to be the call that draws pelagic

108

species. On calm days, we suggest that you just ram your forefinger as far down your throat as you can. This will allow you to call sea birds for the next few seconds. Pace yourself; these calls cannot be repeated too often.

Sometimes the most effective way to call birds is to make a series of rather generic sounds, hoping the bird will respond to one of them. To do this effectively, it is helpful to use a catchy phrase to the tune of a familiar song. We suggest the following procedure:

1. Put two ping pong balls in your mouth.
2. Holding your nose, sing the following lines to the tune of "Happy Birthday":

"Little birdies come here,
little birdies come here,
multi-colored dickey birdies,
little birdies come here."

This call is most effective in heavy underbrush and is unsurpassed in attracting little birdies to your location.

As a note, you can buy a variety of masks to wear while you are making bird calls. These can be quite effective in preventing your friends from recognizing you.

Sand dunes more than 100 feet high change almost instantly into an inland forest at Indian Dunes North Lakeshore in Indiana. Visit in March to catch the migrating raptors, or stay all spring to take in the wide variety of warblers.

Dawn and dusk are the best times to see the 4-foot-tall Sandhill Cranes at Jasper-Pulaski Fish and Wildlife Area, one of Indiana's largest wetlands.

A quarter million Canada Geese call Illinois's Horseshoe Lake Conservation Area home in the winter months. Birders can also see a great variety of wading birds, including Great Blue Herons and rare Yellow-crowned Night Herons.

Great numbers of North America's shorebirds pass through Cheyenne Bottoms Wildlife Area during March, April, and May. Some of the highlights at this Kansas hot spot are Black-necked Stilts, Sandpipers, and the Piping Plover.

Birding in the Central United States

Illinois Beach State Park provides a 6.5-mile stretch of beach along Lake Michigan that is great for bird-watching. The area is frequented by sparrows, hawks, Merlins, and other migratory birds.

Michigan's Whitefish Point Bird Observatory is a prime area for watching the spring and fall migration of raptors and waterfowl. The facility offers bird walks and banding demonstrations during peak spring migration, when you can see 90,000 waterfowl and 20,000 raptors on their way north.

Make way for ducklings! The 61,500 acres in northern Minnesota's Agassiz National Wildlife Refuge offers plenty of space for the 17 species of ducks that nest there every year. Between May and September, visitors are treated to views of up to 25,000 ducklings.

On the shores of Lake Superior, Hawk Ridge Nature Reserve's bluffs provide a perfect view of the rivers of Broad-winged Hawks that travel through during September, along with later fall migrations of Long-eared and Northern Saw-whet Owls.

The largest gathering of cranes in the world happens in March and April at Nebraska's Crane Meadows Nature Center. Visitors can see half a million Sandhill Cranes on the Platte River.

See a thriving population of Sharp-tailed Grouse and the rare Baird's Sparrows at Fort Niobrara National Wildlife Refuge in Nebraska.

North Dakota's Lostwood National Wildlife Refuge produces more ducks than any other state in the lower 48. The 27,000 acres of prairie pothole terrain also produces 49 species of migratory songbirds, 21 species of waterbirds, and much more.

In downtown Columbus, Ohio, visitors will find the Green Lawn Cemetery and Arboretum, a 360-acre haven for both birds and city dwellers complete with a ravine, pond, 3,000 trees, and a butterfly garden. More than 200 species of birds have been spotted there, including 24 different kinds of warblers.

Ohio's Magee Marsh Wildlife Area sees flocks of Blue Jays in spring as well as high concentrations of warblers and other migratory songbirds, though it is also good in other seasons for ducks, swans, rails, and terns.

At the foothills of the Rocky Mountains sits Black Mesa State Park and Nature Preserve in Oklahoma, where birders can see such regional specialties as Pinyon Jays, Mountain Chickadees, Western Kingbirds, and Cassin's Kingbirds.

The bottomland forest in Oklahoma's Little River National Wildlife Refuge features wintering and migrating waterfowl, along with vireos, thrushes, and the difficult-to-spot Swainson's Warbler.

Badlands National Park in South Dakota is a must-see for all, with its grasslands (perfect for raptors and sparrows) and large stone formations. Reintroduced bighorn sheep and bison are also big hits.

The world's largest colony of Franklin's Gulls (around 100,000 pairs) is located at Sand Lake National Wildlife Refuge in South Dakota. The two shallow lakes that make up the preserve are also home to wading birds, shorebirds, and the rare-for-the-area White-faced Ibis.

Wisconsin's Horicon National Wildlife Refuge is the largest freshwater cattail marsh in the United States, which makes it a prime spot for migrating birds, including around one million Canada Geese in autumn. Visit during the Horicon Marsh Birdfest, which takes place during May—peak season for warblers and ducks.

Teddy Roosevelt National Park in North Dakota is a haven for wildlife lovers. Ranging from bison and elk to wild horses and 200 species of birds, the park has breeding Golden Eagles as well as views of Mountain Bluebirds and several varieties of sparrows.

Alexander Wilson

ALEXANDER WILSON, known as the scientific father of American ornithology, was born July 6, 1766, in Paisley, Scotland—an ocean away from the land that would make him famous. As the son of an illiterate Scots distiller, Wilson attended country school until he was old enough to apprentice as a weaver for his brother-in-law. However, the young Wilson was not content to settle for a life as a factory worker and soon left Paisley to wander the countryside.

While intermittently working as a peddler and weaver, Wilson published several books of his own poetry. He wrote mainly about Scottish "low" life—factory workers, farmers, and the poor homesteads he grew up around. Though his work as a poet was never well received, it certainly did not go unnoticed: Wilson was jailed several times for writing pieces that were said to incite local weavers. By 1793, after being released from prison and suffering from a failed love affair, he made the decision to leave Scotland for a new life in America.

117

Arriving penniless in Delaware on July 14, 1794, Wilson took a series of miscellaneous jobs before accepting a position as a schoolteacher in Gray's Ferry, Pennsylvania. His choice of location would prove pivotal. In Gray's Ferry, Wilson's neighbor, William Bartram, was the operator of Bartram Botanical Gardens and a man with an extensive knowledge of and passion for nature. Bartram soon opened his personal library to Wilson and encouraged him to pursue his interest in nature and ornithology.

Not long after being taken under Bartram's wing, Wilson began to take long walks in the countryside as he had in Scotland, but instead of writing poetry he sketched birds. In 1803, after Wilson had walked from his home in Gray's Ferry to Niagara Falls, he felt ready to show his mentor 28 drawings. When he received a positive response, he decided to attempt to publish a collection of his drawings of American birds.

Wilson wrote to an old friend in Scotland, asking him to engrave his first volume. With no financial backing for the project, however, his friend had to decline. Wilson became ever more determined, choosing to leave his job as a schoolteacher and move to Philadelphia. There he took a job as an assistant editor of *Roe's Cyclopedia* for publisher Samuel Bradford. After only a few months under Bradford, Wilson was able to convince his publisher to fund the ornithology book.

In 1808, the first volume of *American Ornithology* was published. Wilson not only created all of the drawings but also supplied most of the text, despite his lack of a formal education. Based entirely on his observations and time in the field, Wilson remarked on the birds' habitats and behaviors. He occasionally changed the European name of a bird when he felt it was not reflective of key elements such as color and habit, or if the name could be applied to many different species of birds.

With each volume being priced at $120, Wilson set out on foot around the East Coast to find subscribers, putting his Scottish peddling experience to the test. Approaching the wealthiest men in each town, the ornithologist and entrepreneur was able to acquire 250 subscribers. On these journeys—which he undertook with each new volume—Wilson collected not only subscribers, but informants and sightings of new species as well. Traveling the eastern coast from Florida to Maine, Wilson met people who would write to him when new birds, migrations, or activity appeared in their area. It was on one of these trips that Alexander Wilson had a chance meeting with a young John James Audubon in Louisville. Though accounts of this meeting differ, many believe Wilson was one of the inspirations for Audubon, who would later publish his own volume of ornithology.

From 1810 to 1813, Wilson published volumes 2 through 7 of *American Ornithology* while living at Bartram's

Botanical Gardens. His personal quest for recognition was coming to fruition with an international reputation as an ornithologist. He gained membership to the Society of Artists of the United States and was admitted into the American Philosophical Society of Philadelphia.

With his eighth volume on waterbirds wrapping up, Wilson turned to work on the ninth, on American quadrupeds. However, the years of traveling the countryside and an earlier bout of dysentery finally caught up with him. In 1813, Wilson took ill with dysentery and passed away.

In his 47 years, Alexander Wilson published seven volumes of *American Ornithology* (with two more following after his death) and illustrated more than 260 species, 26 of which had never been described before. The scientific father of American ornithology has several species named for him, including Wilson's Plover, Wilson's Storm-petrel, and a warbler genus, Wilsonia.

The Jay
By Emily Dickinson

No Brigadier throughout the Year
So civic as the Jay—
A Neighbor and a Warrior too
With shrill felicity
Pursuing Winds that censure us
A February day,
The Brother of the Universe
Was never blown away—
The Snow and he are intimate—
I've often seen them play
When Heaven looked upon us all
With such severity
I felt apology were due
To an insulted sky
Whose pompous frown was Nutriment
To their Temerity—
The Pillow of this daring Head
Is pungent Evergreens—
His Larder—terse and Militant—
Unknown—refreshing things—
His Character—a Tonic—
His Future—a Dispute—
Unfair an Immortality
That leaves this Neighbor out—

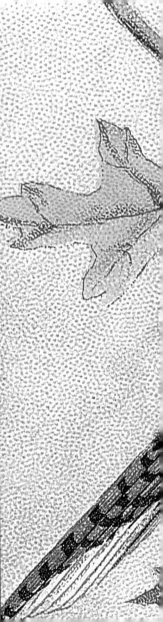

FESTIVALS OF SPRING AND SUMMER

Festivals are a great way to spend a long weekend or that week's vacation you've been saving up while also focusing on your favorite hobby—birdwatching! Meet fellow birders, take in fascinating seminars, and explore the avian community in some of the most beautiful settings Mother Nature has to offer.

April

CELEBRATION OF SWANS
YUKON, CANADA

Yukon's premier bird festival takes place during the third week of April each year. Each community hosts events focused on the beloved Trumpeter Swans as they migrate to the region. Take in a presentation on swan biology, hike to see the swans on Kluane Lake, settle in with the kids for some storytelling, or just go to see the outstanding numbers of swans that migrate to the Yukon.

May

WINGS OVER THE ROCKIES BIRD FESTIVAL
BRITISH COLUMBIA, CANADA

For more than 10 years, bird lovers have been treated to a seven-day festival in the Canadian Rockies. With over 80 educational events to fill your time, the festival will fly by as you take in Voyageur canoe trips, listen to special keynote speakers, participate in a bird-a-thon, and view birds ranging from the Bald Eagle to the Osprey and the Lewis' Woodpecker.

COPPER RIVER DELTA SHOREBIRD FESTIVAL
CORDOVA, AK

If you're looking to take in shorebirds on your vacation, look no farther than this festival in early May. The tidal flats of the Copper River Delta are packed with as many as five million shorebirds resting and feeding here during spring migration.

YOSEMITE BIRDING FESTIVAL
YOSEMITE NATIONAL PARK, CA

The perfect way to gear up for the birding year, this festival begins with a "prologue Outdoor Adventure course" led by an expert who refreshes birders on the best techniques to use in the field. What follows is a full weekend of nonstop birding in the magnificent Yosemite National Park.

UTE MOUNTAIN MESA VERDE BIRDING FESTIVAL
CORTEZ, CO

Enjoy birding the Ute Mountain Tribal Park at all hours during this festival, beginning with a tour to hear the day's first songbird "greet the creators" and ending with a late-night Owl Hoot in which you'll look and listen for a variety of owls.

Birds, Blossoms, and Blues Festival
Norfolk, VA

The Norfolk Botanical Garden packs a lot into its birding celebration, including a blues concert to kick things off. Get your young ones hooked on birding during family classes, shop at the garden market, learn about Virginia's native flora and fauna, and, as always, bird!

Great River Birding & Nature Festival
Lake City, MN

Bird the Mississippi backwaters by motorboat with Audubon guides who can help you find up to 34 warbler species. A slow-moving mini railcar through the Tiffany Wildlife Area stops to let you wander among the nesting Bald Eagles, woodpeckers, and Cuckoos.

Down East Spring Birding Festival
Whiting, ME

This festival centers on the best birding that scenic Maine has to offer, including a trip to Machias Seal Island—one of the finest locations in America to see Atlantic Puffins.

June
Annual Great Adirondack Birding Celebration
Paul Smiths, NY

Spend a weekend birding in the Adirondack regions' lakes, mountains, and bogs. If you're up for a little competition, try the Teddy Roosevelt Birding Challenge, in which you try to find all the birds that TR spotted while in this area.

Bitterroot Birding and Nature Festival
Stevensville, MT

Explore the Bitterroot Valley with more than 35 different guided field trips that allow you to see everything from Black-backed Woodpeckers to Peregrine Falcons and bighorn sheep. Spend your evenings taking in the local culture at the rodeo and chowing down on some BBQ downtown.

August
Sandhill Crane Festival
Fairbanks, AK

Each August, as thousands of Sandhill Cranes begin their southward passage from Alaska and Siberia, the Tanana Valley rings with their calls. This fete includes talks, birdwatching, nature walks, and lots of opportunities for observing cranes and other fall migrants.

Birds sing after a storm; why shouldn't people feel as free to delight in whatever sunlight remains to them?

ROSE KENNEDY

FROM THIS SIMPLE GROVE I have amused myself an hundred times in observing the great number of humming birds with which our country abounds: the wild blossoms everywhere attract the attention of these birds, which like bees subsist by suction. From this retreat I distinctly watch them in all their various attitudes; but their flight is so rapid, that you cannot distinguish the motion of their wings. On this little bird nature has profusely lavished her most splendid colours; the most

FROM LETTERS FROM AN AMERICAN FARMER

BY HECTOR ST. JOHN DE CRÈVECOEUR

perfect azure, the most beautiful gold, the most dazzling red, are for ever in contrast, and help to embellish the plumes of his majestic head. The richest palette of the most luxuriant painter could never invent anything to be compared to the variegated tints, with which this insect bird is arrayed. Its bill is as long and as sharp as a coarse sewing needle; like the bee, nature has taught it to find out in the calix of flowers and blossoms, those mellifluous particles that serve it for sufficient food; and yet it seems to leave them untouched, undeprived of anything that our eyes can possibly distinguish. When it feeds, it appears as if immovable though continually on the wing; and sometimes, from what motives I know not, it will tear and lacerate flowers into a hundred pieces: for, strange to tell, they are the most irascible of the feathered tribe. Where do passions find room in so diminutive a body? They often fight with the fury of lions, until one of the combatants falls a sacrifice and dies. When fatigued, it has often perched within a few feet of me, and on such favourable opportunities I have surveyed it with the most minute attention. Its little eyes appear like diamonds, reflecting light on every side: most elegantly finished in all parts it is a miniature work of our great parent; who seems to have formed it the smallest, and at the same time the most beautiful of the winged species.

Humming-bird

By D. H. Lawrence

I can imagine, in some otherworld
Primeval-dumb, far back
In that most awful stillness, that only gasped
    and hummed,
Humming-birds raced down the avenues.

Before anything had a soul,
While life was a heave of Matter, half inanimate,
This little bit chipped off in brilliance
And went whizzing through the slow, vast,
    succulent stems.

I believe there were no flowers then,
In the world where the humming-bird flashed
    ahead of creation.
I believe he pierced the slow vegetable veins with
    his long beak.

Probably he was big
As mosses, and little lizards, they say, were once big.
Probably he was a jabbing, terrifying monster.

We look at him through the wrong end of the long
    telescope of Time,
Luckily for us.

CONCISE HISTORY OF BIRDING

By Ben, Cathryn, and John Sill

DATE	ACTIVITY	PARTICIPANT COMMENTS
CAVE MAN	Killed birds with rocks	Nice throw, Grog!
DARK AGES	Killed birds by strangulation	My, what a small neck!
RENAISSANCE	Flew tethered birds for sport	Get a longer rope!
VICTORIAN	Put stuffed birds in display cases	Your turn to dust the tern!
1800S	Audubon shot birds to provide pictures drawn "from life"	Bring me more wire!
EARLY 1900S	Ducks "harvested" with long range firearms	Nice shot, Greg!
1930S-40S	Birdwatching with binoculars emerges as a sport; birding barbarianism on the decline	Where is he?
1960S-70S	Bird lists are popular; must see bird to list	Where is he?
1980S-90S	Big Year, Big Day, Big Moment popular; experts use calls to attract birds; don't have to see to list, only hear them	Did you hear that?
BEYOND 2000	Experts compete in calling contests; unnecessary for bird to return the call; points given for technique; Big Call is popular; birds are no longer necessary	Nice call, Grog!

134

Did St. Francis preach to the birds?
Whatever for? If he really liked birds he
would have done better to preach to the cats.

REBECCA WEST

Birding in Canada

- Riding Mountain National Park in Manitoba is the place for birdwatching during nesting season: More than 160 species nest there regularly, including Sprague's Pipits, which perform their courtship displays up in the air above Riding Mountain.

- Enjoy the ferry ride to Grand Manan Archipelago, NB, and take in all the area's 21 islands have to offer, including whales, Razorbills, Atlantic Puffins, Greater Shearwaters, and Common Eiders.

- Long Point, on the shores of Lake Erie in Ontario, has a species list of 360 and has been designated a World Biosphere Site by the United Nations. Spring brings an assortment of migrating warblers and waterfowl, while fall's highlights are the songbirds and hawks that come through.

- Prince Edward Island National Park is perfect for nature lovers. It has extraordinary beaches, red cliffs, and sand dunes, as well as great views of everything from Great Blue Herons to Black Guillemots to Great Cormorants.

- To see the one of two North American Skylark nesting sites, head to Saanich Pennisula, just 10 minutes from downtown Victoria, BC. These birds' numbers have severely dwindled from the 100 pairs that were imported from Great Britain in 1903, so try to make the trip sooner rather than later.

The first Migratory Bird Sanctuary in North America was established at Last Mountain Lake in Saskatchewan after the Migratory Birds Convention Act was passed in 1917. Up to 50,000 cranes, 450,000 geese, and several hundred thousand ducks can be observed when migration peaks.

Outside the town of Oliver, BC, is Vaseux Lake, where Canada's smallest hummingbird, the Calliope, can be found, along with the Golden Eagle. Take a stop at the visitor center to get a full list of waterfowl, which are also abundant here.

THE GIANT HERON

On the shores of the Hudson Bay, a combination of tundra, taiga, coastal, and boreal environments makes Churchill, MB, one of the best places to bird. July is the best time, but come in autumn to see why the town is nicknamed "the Polar Bear Capital of the World."

Gaspé Peninsula in Quebec is a great spot to view all-white nesting Gannets (50,000 of them) as well as stunning Black Guillemots. You can also take in Forillon National Park or go on a boat ride around Percé Rock, which measures more than 2 miles wide and is a favorite place for the shorebirds that cling to the sheer cliff walls.

Point Pelee National Park in Ontario's Carolinian forest attracts birds not typically found in the region, as well as neotropical migrants. With this mix, the species list reaches 370!

To see nesting seabirds up close, look no farther than Cape St. Mary's Ecological Reserve in Newfoundland. Take walking trails to the rocks where, during the breeding season, 24,000 Gannets, 20,000 Black-legged Kittiwakes, 20,000 Common Murres, and 2,000 Thick-billed Murres make their home.

The Queen Charlotte Islands in British Columbia are a haven for pelagic birdwatching. Enjoy a day cruise while spotting different species of alcids, loons, cormorants, and gulls.

The Loon Upon the Lake

Ojibwa Song

I looked across the water,
    I bent o'er it and listened,
I thought it was my lover,
    My true lover's paddle glistened.
Joyous thus his light canoe would the silver ripples
    wake.
But no!—it is the loon alone—the loon upon the lake.
Ah me! it is the loon alone—the loon upon the lake.

I see the fallen maple
    Where he stood, his red scarf waving,
Though waters nearly bury
    Boughs they then were newly laving.
I hear his last farewell, as it echoed from the brake.—
But no, it is the loon alone—the loon upon the lake.
Ah me! it is the loon alone—the loon upon the lake

142

John and Elizabeth Gould

KNOWN BY SOME as "the Bird Man," John Gould came to earn his reputation years after he was born on the Dorset coast of England at Lyme Regis in 1804. Gould's father was a gardener who worked on an estate near Guildford, Surrey, and in 1818 became foreman at the Royal Gardens of Windsor. This exposure to gardening provided young Gould with an early education about birds based purely on his outdoor experience and observation. In fact, he was never formally trained at college and in adulthood considered himself a self-made man.

As a youth Gould trained under his father to be a gardener, picking up the trade of taxidermy along the way. In 1824, he moved to London and opened his own taxidermy business. He became the first curator and preserver at the museum of the Zoological Society of London in 1827. This position put Gould in contact with Great Britain's leading naturalists, and often gave him a first look at new collections of birds given to the society from all over the world.

144

In 1830, a collection of birds arrived from the Himalayas, many of which Gould had never seen described in any literature or research. He illustrated these birds in the volume *A Century of Birds from the Himalayas*. John's wife Elizabeth Coxen Gould, who was an accomplished artist prior to their marriage in 1829, lithographed the illustrations. She went on to become the chief artist and lithographer in the Gould partnership for its first 10 years of major publications. In the succeeding years, they produced—together with lithographer Edward Lear—*The Birds of Europe*, *A Monograph of the Ramphastidae*, and *A Monograph of the Trogonidae*, among others.

In 1837, Charles Darwin presented mammal and bird specimens collected during his voyage on the HMS *Beagle* to the Geological Society of London. The bird specimens were given to Gould for identification, and after six days he was confident the birds from the Galapagos Islands Darwin thought were blackbirds, grosbeaks, and finches were actually "a series of ground Finches which are so peculiar," he wrote, as to form "an entirely new group, containing 12 species." This of course was breaking news, and Darwin and Gould together determined that the species differed from island to island, each unique, a critical step in the development of Darwin's theory of evolution.

The following year, the Goulds sailed to Australia with the intent to study, research, and publish subsequent volumes of their work. They stayed for two years, and in that time John traveled extensively—as far as 400 miles into the interior of the continent, an expedition that claimed the lives of two of his assistants. Elizabeth gave birth to the first of three sons at the Government House in Hobart, Tasmania. On the journey, she completed many paintings, which are dated, signed, and part of the Gould Collection. Upon their return they published *The Birds of Australia*, which included 600 lithograph illustrations in seven volumes, 328 of which were new to modern science and named by Gould.

Unfortunately, Elizabeth died the following year, in 1841, having contributed greatly to her husband's life work. Her art was translated into lithographs by H. C. Richter and published under his name.

Throughout his professional life, Gould had a particular fascination with hummingbirds. Over the years, he accumulated a collection of 320 species, but had never seen a living specimen. In 1857 he traveled with his son Charles to the United States in order to see a live hummingbird. It was in Philadelphia, in Bartram's Gardens, that Gould saw his first live hummingbird, a Ruby-throated. In Washington, DC, father and son saw a large number of hummingbirds in the gardens of the Capitol. Gould appreciated their beauty so much that he attempted to return to England with live birds. He did not understand completely the conditions necessary to sustain them, however, so each lived for only a month or two.

To honor his significant contribution to science in Australia, the country founded the Gould League in 1909. This organization went on to give many Australians their first introduction to birding, along with more general environmental and ecological education.

Pale Male, the Red-tailed hawk that is the first ever known to nest on a building rather than in a tree, has made its home atop a building on Fifth Avenue in New York City for years. An avid group of New York hawk-watchers wait to see if Pale Male's three chicks will survive their first flight off the ledge and into Central Park.

FROM

RED-TAILS IN LOVE

BY MARIE WINN

A FLEDGLING VIGIL was organized, with volunteers scheduled to be at the hawk bench from 6:00 a.m. to 7:00 p.m. in case disaster struck. Charles Kennedy usually took the sunrise slot, arriving by bike from his Soho loft. He brought a blanket for throwing over a fallen fledgling and a whistle for stopping traffic.

Crowds began to gather at the model-boat pond as the time for fledging approached. The stalwarts arrived at sunrise, their ranks swelled as the day went on, and by evening hundreds would be lining up at the numerous telescopes, hoping to see a hawk baby fledge.

As at all New York events, the TV news folks came around. ABC News managed to get their cameras on a terrace of the building just south of the nest building, the one hawkwatchers referred to as the Ugly White Condo. It looked directly into the nest, allowing

151

the cameraman to get remarkable close-up shots of the young hawks jumping up and down and running from side to side.

A Fledging Pool was organized, and everyone threw two dollars into the pot to buy a two-hour slot. Sharon Freedman signed up for June 2nd, from noon to 2:00 p.m. It was her birthday, and she was determined to win. At 10:30 that morning, as the largest of the babies was flapping especially hard, she called out: "Don't go now! Too early." The bird obediently quieted down and settled in for a rest. In fact, nobody fledged that day, or the next.

Now the hawkwatchers began to wonder if those babies would *ever* leave. Various theories were proposed about what would finally get them going: (1) hunger (if the parents stopped feeding them); (2) the stench of leftover prey and the misery of parasites in the nest; (3) the right weather conditions, with the wind blowing from the east to help them across the street; (4) a surge of courage; (5) the joy of flying. Perhaps it was a combination of all of these that finally did it.

It happened on June 4th, a Sunday. That morning at church Barbara Ascher said a prayer for the baby hawks (and for the hawkwatchers too). She didn't know that the first bird had already flown by the time she got there, but it may have helped retroactively—who knows how prayers work.

152

It began:

> Dear God, Thank you for hawks
> That have made us more than we were.
> Thank you for opening our hearts.
> As their shells opened, so did ours.

And it ended:

> Help us to accept, although we pray that they find safe perches.
> And God, we pray especially this night for the first to fly....

Tom Fiore, to nobody's surprise, was the only one there when the first of the three nestlings took off. Something had told him this would be the day, and he decided to get to the model-boat pond even earlier than usual. He got there at 5:35 a.m., just around sunrise. He reported:

> When I arrived at the boat pond, all three nestlings were up. They were all facing front and sitting perfectly still. Anthropomorphically speaking, they were anticipating a meal. Maybe they were looking for the other hawkwatchers—Where's Charles? After five minutes they started flapping and jumping.

They seemed to be alternating, first one, then another jumped and flapped. This went on for about fifteen minutes. Then the one on the north side started flapping again. He lifted up and I thought, "Uh-oh, this is a pretty good hop." And then he kept on going! He looked a little awkward but he didn't go down. He just flew straight north. He flapped right by Woody's. Then he got to the next building, the one with the big green shade, and landed on the ledge at the top. He folded his wings and looked down and around, as if to say: "Uh-oh, what do I do now?"

I arrived at 6:00 a.m. Three minutes too late! Charles Kennedy arrived two minutes later. Damn! Still, our disappointment was mitigated by relief at the fledgling's success and admiration for his bravery. We could see him there on the Green Shade Building and agreed that the bird was almost certainly a male. For one thing, he looked small, and besides, the first to leave are generally the males, according to Palmer. We watched fledger #1 practice flying skills by taking short, flying jumps from one level of the building to another, maneuvering the landings with his wings. It was as if he were in a tree hopping from branch to branch just like the Trostles' fledglings in Logan, Utah. An enterprising urban hawk.

Birdwatching is a sport, a hobby, a skilled occupation. Hawkwatching

154

is an obsession. Like love, it exhilarates. Like love, it brings anxiety. Birdwatchers watch and listen, ever in hope of something exciting just around the corner. Hawkwatchers exult and despair.

By 5:00 a.m. on June 5th, a small crowd had already gathered at the hawk bench, hoping to see the next baby take off. Obviously nothing was going to happen—Tom Fiore wasn't there, someone noted jealously. Marcia Lowe had taken half a Valium to quell anxiety. Patricia Miller, another devoted hawkwatcher, said she'd been up all night worrying about the fledgling's first night out on his own. She had circles under eyes.

Anxiety turned into hysteria a little after noon. Fledger, as yesterday's hero had been named, had spent most of the day on top of Woody's water tower, and to the hawkwatchers' concerned eyes he didn't seem happy. "Something's the matter with him. He doesn't look right," said Holly. "He hasn't eaten all day. I think he's starving," said Marcia. Blanche was weeping quietly.

When a large group of tourists on a Suzi's Specialty Tour passed by the hawk bench, Merrill asked if they wanted to see a baby hawk. Thirty-three visitors from Wisconsin lined up and looked at Fledger on the water tower. Then they lined up again to look at the two babies jumping up and down in the nest. They quickly absorbed some of our anxiety and wanted to stay and see if one of the parents came with food for the baby. But Suzi (or a reasonable facsimile) firmly herded them off to their next destination: the Dakota, where *Rosemary's Baby* was filmed and John Lennon was assassinated.

By midafternoon, to everyone's relief, Fledger left his perch on the water tower and began to check out the neighborhood. First he flew to the Ugly White Condo, then to the roof of the nest building itself, and finally to an air conditioner on the Octagonal Building at 75th and Fifth.

Red-tails glide and soar: flap-flap — glide — glide. But Fledger flew like a crow on his first day out of the nest: flap-flap-flap-flap. Mostly, however, he didn't fly at all: He waddled or sidled along the edges of each building he landed on. Sometimes he hopped up and down as he had done in the nest. But out in the world, instead of landing back in the same place, he gave an extra wing push and landed on the next floor, ending up awkwardly balanced on a railing, or planter, or ornamental statue on someone's well-appointed terrace. At each new location he behaved like young creatures generally do: He poked around and explored. Sometimes he simply collapsed in a little heap and had a nap, whether on a ledge or a windowsill.

Around 4:00 p.m., as Fledger perched on top of the Octagonal Building, his father suddenly appeared in the air directly above him and proceeded to demonstrate the art of flying like a red-tailed hawk. Elegantly, the pale bird soared and circled, first toward the Metropolitan Museum of Art where some of the choicest pigeons hang out, then back past the Octagonal Building where the fledgling was watching with raptorly attention, then on toward 72nd Street, then to Pilgrim Hill, where some of the tastiest rats may be found. Finally, he flew back to the Octagonal Building, circled Fledger two more times, and concluded the lesson, landing on the balcony just under the nest. There we could see the remaining two baby hawks in the nest, quietly watching.

Fledger got the idea right away. Hardly had his old man settled down on the next building when he took off and flew an entire city block to Woody's building without a single flap. All glide. Once again the crowd at the boat pond cheered. "Bellissimo," said an Italian tourist. "Unglaublich," uttered a German visitor—unbelievable.

So far the young hawk had spent his entire life in, or rather on, apartment houses. Unlike most New Yorkers, he had yet to experience the delicious relief Central Park offers the city dweller. On the afternoon of his third day in the wide world, a few minutes before

4:00 p.m., Fledger left his perch on Woody's water tower and sailed into the park.

Jay Sharff, another devoted hawkwatcher, and Marcia had been at the hawk bench since sunrise—they were running on nervous energy. Now they screamed as they saw the bird disappear into the park. They raced from the hawk bench past the Alice in Wonderland statue, following the sound of shrieking blue jays—an excellent indication of a hawk in the neighborhood.

They found Fledger in a red oak. He was sitting near the top of the tree, swaying a bit in the breeze. It was surely the first time in his life that his perch moved under his feet and he seemed puzzled. His life as a tree-dwelling red-tailed hawk had just begun.

On June 6th at 6:08 a.m., with the usual crowd of morning observers in attendance, the second fledgling took off. Amid the hawkwatchers' excited cries, the bird flew toward the Green Shade Building, headed for the windowsill of the top-floor apartment (the one with the green shade), couldn't figure out how to land, fumbled around a few other windows, and finally flew toward the park, disappearing below the tree line.

"Oh my God, he crashed on Fifth Avenue," someone shouted. Everyone rushed toward the 76th Street park entrance and out onto

Fifth. Charles was prepared to stop traffic. For just such a contingency he had tucked a red T-shirt in his backpack. It would serve as a flag. His traffic-cop whistle was in his pocket.

We looked up and down Fifth Avenue—no bird in sight. Then we heard a sound that instantly lifted our spirits: loud blue jay clamor in the park. Back into the park we raced, heading in the direction of the hopeful sound. There, in a pin oak tree just one tree east of Fledger's landing site the day before, we saw the second fledgling. We recognized the baby hawk immediately. It was the one with the reddish chest. Somebody began to call it Lucy—after the redhead of TV fame, I suppose—and the name stuck, though Lucy was quite probably a male.

There must have been a blue jay nest in Lucy's landing tree—the jays were going berserk. They were dive-bombing the fledgling and he did not look happy. He had just left the perfect protection of the nest, and now this! Then, to our deep delight . . . Pale Male to the rescue. For the last hour he had been perched on the top railing of the Octagonal Building, supervising. Seeming to be in no hurry, he floated off and sailed, one might say he aerially sauntered toward the tree where the fledgling was sitting, all hunched up, trying to deflect the blue jay blows. Lucy's father flew by the tree once, then turned and flew by again in the other direction. He was flying low, at Baby's eye level. As he passed Lucy's pin oak, he uttered a cry we had little trouble understanding. "Kreeeeuuur," we heard. "You did good, kid. Don't worry about those jays. They can't really hurt you. Just hang in there and I'll bring lunch soon."

By the evening of June 6th each of the first two fledglings had returned from the park to the more familiar precincts of man-made structures. With the warm glow of the sun in the west illuminating the Fifth Avenue skyline, one young hawk could be seen perched on a balcony of the apartment just under Woody's, and the other on the roof of the Octagonal Building. Though they were out of earshot, through binoculars the watchers at the hawk bench could plainly see the fledglings' beaks opening and closing regularly: They were crying, just like babies.

Two out—one more to go. Just before noon on June 7th, Jane Koryn witnessed the last fledging. An addicted hawkwatcher who lived in Woody's building, during the entire fledging vigil Jane took it upon herself to bring trays of buttery Danish pastries and a large thermos of fresh coffee to the early morning contingent at the hawk bench. I remember arriving very early one morning and watching for the light to go on in Jane's kitchen. Coffee coming soon. From her twelfth-

160

floor living-room window Jane could easily see the balconies of the nest apartment. She could see the nest too, but only by leaning way, way out of her window. One fact is clear from her report: She wasn't getting much sleep those days. As she described it to me shortly after the events:

Last night I looked out after dinner and Mom was sitting on the balcony at the north end of the hawk apartment. I checked at 10:30 p.m. and then again at 1:30 a.m.—she was still there. At 6:00 this morning as I was heading for the hawk bench she was still in the same spot. She didn't leave for four and a half hours.

Pale Male brought something to eat into the nest at 10:30 a.m. A few minutes later I ran to the window because I heard hawk sounds. I could see a lot of activity. Both parents flew by the nest a couple of times, and then circled nearby. Then both the previously fledged babies flew by. I could hear the one that was still in the nest calling—it was the one that still had a few white fuzzy feathers on its head. Then I heard one of the brothers or sisters call as it flew by the nest: Come join us! This is fun! For around fifteen minutes all four—Mom and Dad and the two fledglings—were flying around. Then the parent hawks perched on the black smokestack and had a powwow.

There was a wonderful breeze for the next half hour. It finally happened a few minutes before noon. When the last baby left it flew perfectly, as if it were an adult. It flew right into the park.

And now the reality is sinking in. I still can't believe it. We have an empty nest.

Everyone turned out for the Fledge party—hawkwatchers, Regulars, Fifth Avenue neighbors, hangers-out at the model-boat pond, park employees, park characters—hawk lovers all.

As the party began, the thought of an end ever coming to their fellowship of hawkwatchers made everyone gloomy. That's when Dorothy Poole offered to lead a weekly walk in the Ramble for those who wanted to learn about birds and trees and flowers and butterflies, a walk in all seasons to follow the natural cycles in Central Park. It would have to be early in the morning, for Dorothy had a job, and so, indeed, did some of the hawkwatchers enthusiastic about the idea. It was the beginning of the Earlybirds, a birdwatching group that goes on to this day.

As ever at bird celebrations everyone brought an offering of food or drink, and as the goodies were unpacked, spirits lifted considerably. Charles Kennedy brought a hazelnut cake from the Cupcake Café, his favorite bakery. It bore an icing picture of a noble hawk with outstretched wings and a bright red tail. Though no red-tailed hawk in history had ever had a tail that red—it was the brilliant red of a ripe tomato—the portrait was universally admired. But only

162

briefly; the delicate, buttery cake disappeared quickly.

Jane Koryn brought cookies from a famous bakery on Madison Avenue. Regina Alvarez, the zone gardener for the model-boat pond area, baked a corn cake. Tom brought apples and grapes. Dorothy Poole brought Hawk Crest wine. The Girards and Mo and Sylvia brought home-made appetizers. Nora brought paper cups, plates, and cider.

For the climactic toast Blanche Williamson brought out two bottles of Veuve Clicquot-Ponsardin—the real thing! Weren't we as classy as the hawk building people any day?

Be Like the Bird
By Victor Hugo

Be like the bird, who
Halting in his flight
On limb too slight
Feels it give way beneath him,
Yet sings
Knowing he hath wings.

Creating a Backyard Bird Haven

WHETHER YOU'RE STARTING your garden from scratch or your interest in birding has inspired you to plant a more bird-friendly yard, the first thing to do is think big. Birds need trees, shrubs, and vines that provide shelter from the elements year-round. And the best way to provide good nesting opportunities and shelter is with evergreens: pines, cedars, spruces, yews, and junipers. The thing to keep in mind with evergreens is that most grow to be very tall, so make sure you plant them in the back, in the corners, or along the borders of your garden. Again, evergreens offer the best of everything year-round for your favorite feathered friends, so plan for about 10 percent of your garden to be made up of this kind of plant.

Another must-have for every birder's garden is the tried-and-true birdbath. Options abound when picking out a birdbath and deciding where to place it, but one type in particular will draw the crowds you're looking for: the drip bath. Birds are strongly attracted to dripping water; this addition to your yard will bring in warblers, flycatchers, northern thrushes, and other migrating birds that probably wouldn't otherwise stop. The easiest way to rig up your drip bath is to place it beneath a sturdy overhanging branch that can support a small wooden bucket. Drill a hole into the bottom of the bucket—keep it small enough so that it releases a single droplet every one to two seconds—and arrange it on the limb so that it rests about two feet above the surface of the birdbath. The continued drips will attract all kinds!

The plant—or weed, depending on whom you ask—known as pokeberry, pokeweed, poke, scoke, garget, or redweed is one of the very best for bringing birds to your garden. The only problem is how unattractive the plant itself is! Still, if you're willing to tuck it away into a corner and maintain it so your garden isn't overrun, you'll find that it works wonders for your avian visitors. Pokeberry grows best in sunny, moist places like along the edge of your fence. While it's hard to find at your local nursery, because so many folks consider it a weed, birds often plant it themselves by dropping seeds in flight. Species that particularly favor the pokeberry include Mourning Doves, bluebirds, catbirds, woodpeckers, robins, mockingbirds, thrushes, vireos, and cardinals.

North American birds crave different types of berries and plants. Here are some simple garden additions you can plant to attract various favorite species:

- Bluebirds, cardinals, and catbirds: blackberries, wild cherries, dogwoods, wild grapes, cedars or junipers, mulberries, Virginia creeper, sumacs, blueberries, elderberries, hollies, and bayberries.
- Chickadees: pines, oaks, maples, spruces, Virginia creeper, blueberries, birches, elms, hemlocks, serviceberries, firs, bayberries, and sweet gum.
- Purple Finches: dogwoods, cedars or junipers, maples, sumacs, black gum, elms, tulip tree, ashes, aspens, and sweet gum.
- Goldfinches: maples, elms, tulip tree, alders, and sweet gum.
- Mockingbirds: blackberries, dogwoods, wild grapes, cedars, junipers, mulberries, Virginia

creeper, sumacs, black gum,
elderberries, serviceberries,
greenbriers, hollies, hackberries,
palmettos, persimmons,
manzanitas, and California
pepper tree.

Warblers: pines, blackberries,
dogwoods, wild grapes, cedars,
junipers, mulberries, sumacs,
elderberries, and persimmons.

Orioles: blackberries,
mulberries, blueberries, elderberries, and serviceberries.

Vireos: blackberries, wild
cherries, dogwoods, wild
grapes, Virginia creeper, sumacs,
elderberries, bayberries, wild
roses, and snowberries.

There is nothing in which
the birds differ more from
man than the way in which
they can build and yet leave a
landscape as it was before.

ROBERT LYND

Phoebe Snetsinger

PHOEBE SNETSINGER WAS the most prolific birder in history, which is an exceptional feat for someone who didn't begin birding seriously until she was 50 years old. She defined a specific group of new birders who had the financial freedom to travel anywhere to see a rare bird, hiring the best tour guides to get them there. The story of how she came to birding, and how quickly her dedication grew, is a testament to what can happen when one is bitten by the bug.

Born in 1931 in Lake Zurich, Illinois, Snetsinger attended a one-room elementary schoolhouse and was involved with 4-H Club, where she met her future husband at age 11. The Snetsingers had four children, and it wasn't until 1965 that she went birding for the first time, when a friend in Minnesota took her out to see her first

173

Blackburnian Warbler. After that, Snetsinger joined a local group of amateur birders in her area who took walks every Thursday. But only in 1981 did she turn to birding with a passion.

At age 50, Snetsinger was diagnosed with melanoma and told by her doctor that she had less than a year to live. Instead of undergoing therapy, Snetsinger decided to join a birding trip to Alaska—a decision that would radically affect her life for her remaining 18 years. Following Alaska, Snetsinger found herself on a three-week trip to Kenya, where she saw 500 different birds. It was this experience that truly sparked her desire to see as many birds as she could.

Soon, using her modest inheritance, Snetsinger was off on trips all over the globe. Before each journey she did a remarkable amount of research, learning not only about the birds she would be looking for but also the geology and general ecology of the area. Once at her destination, she relied on guides to take her deep into often dangerous and unknown places. She birded on all seven continents, seeing a Rock-hopper Penguin in the Falkland Islands and more than 400 species in Australia. She was shipwrecked and attacked, she survived injuries and earthquakes, but she never thought of quitting. Even as her cancer went in and out of remission, Snetsinger fought to continue what avid birders call "the game."

Snetsinger's compulsion to bird led her to an interesting focus: monotypic genera, a large group of genera that each contains but one species. Her final tally was more than 2,000 monotypic genera, far beyond anyone else's list. In 1999, at age 68, Snetsinger was in Madagascar on a birding expedition. The group had just seen a rare Helmet Vanga when there was a van accident; Snetsinger was killed instantly. Eighteen years after receiving a fatal diagnosis, the world's most famous "lister" had sighted around 8,400 birds—approximately one new species every single day. Her passion has left a lasting legacy within the birding community and especially among her children, three of whom are now working in the field of ornithology.

The Red Kite is a graceful, slow-flying bird of prey found over much of Europe. Both males and females have quite a varied appetite, dining on a range of prey from earthworms to sheep carrion (but only when a larger bird comes along to open up the carcass first!).

Breeding throughout Greenland and northern Eurasia, the White-tailed Eagle experiences a shaky early development period. Although the

Birds of Europe

birds are capable of taking care of themselves after only 30 days, they will continue to beg for food from adults. In the end, 60 or 70 percent fail to survive their first year after leaving the nest.

White Wagtails—found across Europe in the warm months—are known for their constant *chirrup* in city parks and countryside. Once a cave or cliff dweller, this bird now makes its home in the eaves of houses, using layer after layer of mud to create a nest with an opening small enough to keep House Sparrows out.

The Red-backed Shrike is a songbird with predator-like eating habits. Dining on large insects, small birds, voles, and lizards across Europe from Britain to Siberia, the shrike hunts from prominent perches and impales prey on thorns or barbed wire.

Although its name suggests that it may be a good swimmer, the White-throated Dipper only rarely dives or walks into water. The name is instead attributed to the bird's habit of bobbing spasmodically while perched on rocks near running water in the mountainous regions of Europe.

Female Dunnocks, found throughout most of Europe in woodland, shrub, and gardens, breed with two males at once, thus giving rise to great competition for mating access to the female. DNA testing has shown that chicks within the same brood often have different fathers.

The countryside wouldn't be complete without a few Barn Owls. In northern England, owl broth was once given to sufferers of whooping cough because their strained wheezing was similar to the sounds of an owl.

Northern Lapwings can be found on farmland throughout Europe, and are distinctive with their thin black crests. Their scientific name—*Vanellus vanellus*—means "little fan" and describes the birds' slow flight.

The European Robin is a smart scavenger. It will often approach gardeners as they work to reap any food turned up in the soil. European Robins in the wild will do the same, approaching large animals such as wild boars to investigate the disturbed ground for any food that might be brought to the surface.

The Scottish Crossbill is the only bird endemic to the United Kingdom. Found only in the Scottish Highlands in established Scotch pine trees (young trees don't produce cones), it eats pine seeds and can be seen year-round.

BIRDING AT THE MOVIES

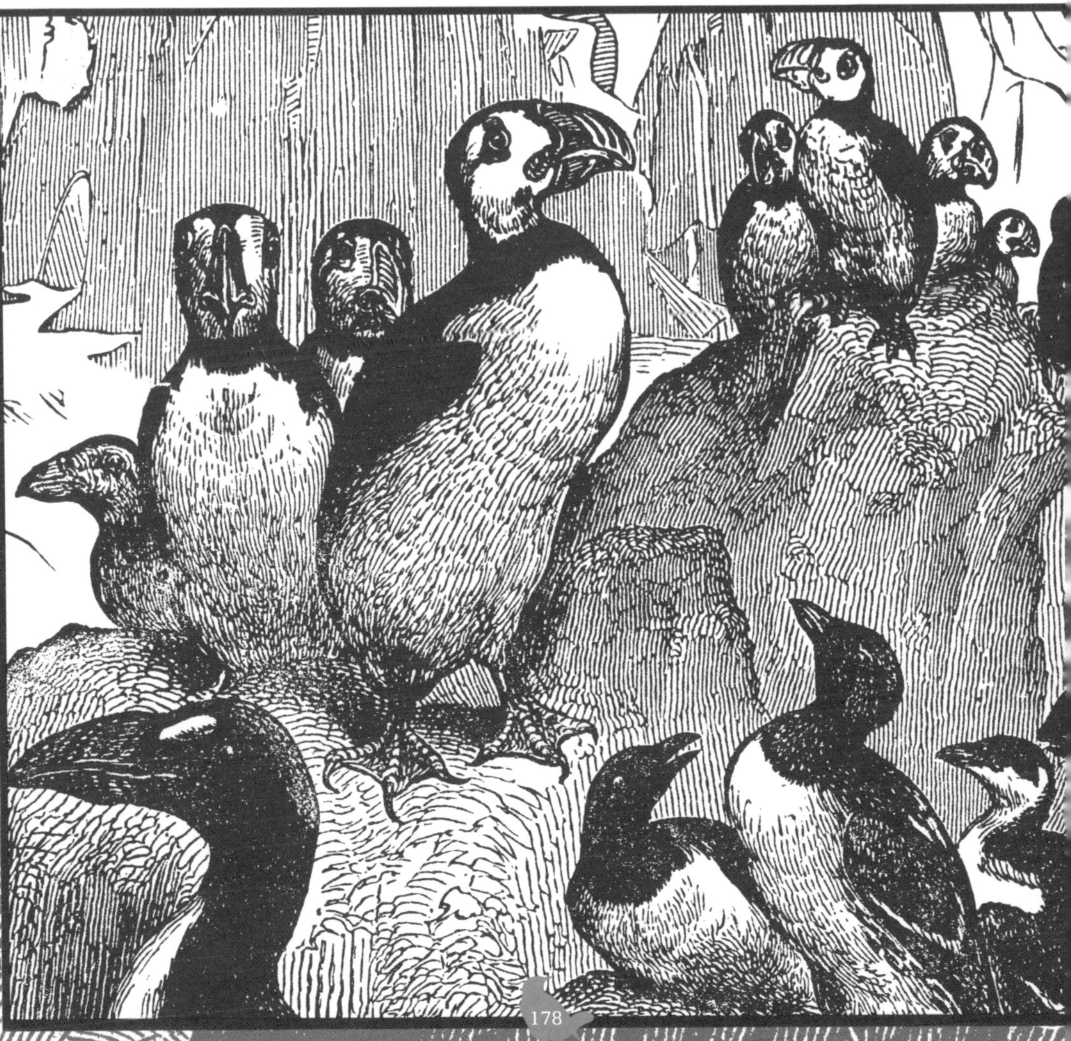

Are you seriously addicted to birds? Do you spend your non-birding free time in online forums discussing optics, or in your woodshop carving the birds you saw that day? Then post this list on your refrigerator as must-rent flicks for the next time you head to the video store.

Adventures in Birdwatching (2004). Join ornithologist Ken Dial as he travels to birding hot spots from Costa Rica to Washington State, incorporating humor and valuable information along the way.

Bill Oddie's How to Watch Wildlife (2006). Featuring birds as well as other wildlife, BBC's favorite naturalist travels the UK during all four seasons, demonstrating how to find and understand fauna.

The Birds (1963). Sure, it might not be the most positive account of birds, but for anyone who as a child stood on a beach trying to feed one adorable seagull only to be swarmed by hundreds, it certainly is a true testament to a specific bird experience. Besides, who can say no to a Hitchcock film?

Birds Birds Birds: An Indoor Field Trip (2005). If you are feeling under the weather but still want to keep up your birding skills, try this indoor field trip, which focuses primarily on knowing your birdsongs. Eighteen quizzes help you brush up on your knowledge.

Fly Away Home (1996). Based loosely on a true story, this movie tells the tale of a young girl and her eccentric inventor father attempting to save a flock of young geese that need to be guided south for their first winter.

The Life of Birds (1998). This 10-part, five-volume series is hosted by famed British naturalist David Attenborough and takes viewers around the globe examining bird behavior.

March of the Penguins (2005). Winner of the Academy Award for Best Documentary Feature, this film follows the grueling journey of Antarctica's Empire Penguins to their breeding grounds and biggest challenge—incubating their egg during the bleak and brutal winter.

Pale Male (2002). From the PBS series *Nature*, this is the story of a Red-tailed Hawk named Pale Male who made his home on the ledge of an exclusive Fifth Avenue apartment building in the center of Manhattan and became an instant celebrity.

The Wild Parrots of Telegraph Hill (2003). A documentary about a homeless musician in San Francisco who befriends a flock of red and green parrots around Telegraph Hill.

Winged Migration (2001). In this Academy Award–nominated documentary, cameras follow bird migrations from North America to the Arctic over four years using new technology to get the viewer in at the birds' level.

UP FROM THE EGG:
CONFESSIONS OF A NUTHATCH AVOIDER

By Ogden Nash

Bird watchers top my honors list.
I aimed to be one, but I missed.
Since I'm both myopic and astigmatic,
My aim turned out to be erratic,
And I, bespectacled and binocular,
Exposed myself to comment jocular.
We don't need too much birdlore, do we,
To tell a flamingo from a towhee;
Yet I cannot, and never will,
Unless the silly birds stand still.
And there's no enlightenment in a tour
Of ornithological literature.
Is yon strange creature a common chickadee,
Or a migrant alouette from Picardy?
You can rush to consult your Nature guide
And inspect the gallery inside,
But a bird in the open never looks
Like its picture in the birdie books—
Or if it once did, it has changed its plumage,
And plunges you back into ignorant gloomage.
That is why I sit here growing old by inches,
Watching a clock instead of finches,
But I sometimes visualize in my gin
The Audubon that I audubin.

John James Audubon

John James Audubon was a self-taught artist and naturalist whose drawings and watercolors of American birds continue to influence avian artists today. Born in 1785 on the small island of Santo Domingo (now Haiti), he was the illegitimate son of Captain Jean Audubon, a sailor, merchant, and plantation owner. His mother, a chambermaid, died shortly after his birth. Audubon was sent to France to live with his father's wealthy wife, who raised him as one of her own children. During his youth in Nantes, Audubon developed a fascination with the natural world and spent his free time observing and sketching the wildlife around him.

When Audubon turned 18, he was sent to the United States to learn English, attend to his father's estate in Mill Grove, Philadelphia, and avoid conscription by the Napoleonic army. While in Pennsylvania, Audubon began a series of experiments including one of the first bird-banding programs, with migrating Eastern Phoebes. By noting that the returning birds wore his strings, he was able to deduce that they came back to the same nesting sites each year. His avian drawings continued to improve during this time, as he invented a more effective way of posing specimens by placing wires through the dead birds.

After selling his father's estate, Audubon and his wife, Lucy Bakewell, moved to Louisville to establish a general store. Though initially successful in business, the Audubon family was forced to relocate several times due to the lack of financial opportunities, and at age 34, Audubon was briefly imprisoned on bankruptcy charges. When released from jail, the amateur painter returned to his art in order to support his family, working for a time at the Western Museum as a taxidermist and habitat painter while running a small art school on the side.

In 1820, Audubon decided it was time to follow the dream he had been fostering for more than 15 years and began to travel down the Mississippi, studying and drawing birds. Bringing with him only his artist's materials, an assistant, and a gun, he left Lucy to support the family on her wages earned from tutoring wealthy plantation owners. (It was through this connection that the Audubon Society came to be named, for although Audubon never played a part in the avian organization, one of its founders was tutored by Lucy Audubon and used the artist as inspiration for the group's earliest work in bird protection.)

When Audubon returned from his trip, he tried desperately to market his works, but his rugged style, greased hair, and lack of educational credentials made potential publishers uncomfortable. Unable to find interest in America, Audubon

urned to England. In 1826, he took his finished works across
he Atlantic, where his mountaineer looks were considered
captivating. He became an overnight success, nicknamed "the
American Woodsman," and his collection of essays and intricate,
ife-size drawings became the first edition of *The Birds of America*
and later the *Ornithological Biography*.

In 1829, after several successful volumes were published,
he artist returned to the United States, where he continued to
ravel, collect, and paint specimens on and off as he published
works. One of his last expeditions was to the upper Missouri
River and the Dakotas, where he was determined to finish his
next major project, *Viviparous Quadrupeds of North America.* During
he 1840s, however, he began to lose his eyesight. In 1851, he
uffered from a stroke and subsequently passed away at his New
York estate at the age of 66.

During his life, Audubon faced criticism for many
hings: the lack of sophistication of his work, his use of paper
or his art, and his tendency to exaggerate his training and
accomplishments. More than a century and a half later, though,
Audubon is best remembered for his passion for the American
avian, his persistence in following his dream, and his later
writings on the conservation of avian habitats, which have
nspired thousands of ornithologists, artists, and nature lovers.

A LITTLE COMMON SENSE:

WHERE COMMON NAMES ORIGINATED

We can all understand why a bluebird is called a bluebird, but where did the common names *Coffin-bearer* or *Goatsucker* come from? Though there are often several theories as to where common names originated, here are some of generally accepted reasons why we call a brown-colored bird a Cherry, and so on.

- The Baltimore Oriole was named by Mark Catesby in 1731. He chose the name because the bird's colors were the same as those of the Baltimores, who were the colonial proprietors of Maryland.

- The name *Basketbird* (Northern Oriole) refers to the woven nests it makes.

- A Bee-bird or Bee-martin (Kingbird) is known for taking bees from their hive.

- Bellbirds (Wood Thrushes) have a song "clear as a bell" that "rings" out.

- Butcher-birds (Shrike) impale their food in order to eat it.

The Calliope Hummingbird was named after one of the nine muses: Calliope, the muse of epic poetry. Unlike an epic, however, this hummingbird is the smallest of its kind.

Wild Canaries (American Goldfinch or Yellow Warbler) looked similar to the caged birds that were brought to Italy from the Canary Islands during the 16th century.

A Cherry Bird (Cedar Waxwing) loves wild cherries, and is often seen squeezing the juice into the mouths of its youngsters.

The Coffin-bearer (Great Black-backed Gull) has a slow and deliberate style of walking, as if it's in mourning.

An explanation for the Crossbill's distinctive beak is found in religious legend. According to one story, the bill became crossed after the bird tried to pull out the nails that held Jesus to the cross. The red plumage comes from Christ's blood.

The Devil Downhead gained its name from its Evel Knievel behavior of traveling down a tree trunk headfirst.

The name *flamingo* is from the Latin *flamma*, meaning "flame," after its bright plumage.

Aristotle perpetuated the legend surrounding the Goatsucker (Whip-poor-will), saying that it drank from the udder of goats and caused the animals to go blind.

Barnacle Goose is from an old superstition stating these birds hatched from the shellfish that were attached to shipwrecks deep in the sea.

The Limpkin gets its name from its less-than-graceful walk, which suggests a limp.

The Magnolia Warbler was named by Alexander Wilson, who shot his first specimen in a magnolia tree.

The term *nuthatch* can be broken into *nut* and *hatch*—the latter derived, in turn, from *hack*. This bird is often seen forcing nuts into small spaces and hacking them until they're small enough to swallow.

The Ovenbird (Warbler or Family Furnariidae) makes a nest in the forest floor or out of clay that looks much like a small oven.

Pheasants were named after their habitat near the River Phasis.

The American Cuckoo, or Rain Bird, has a call that was thought to foretell rain.

The Ruffed Grouse has tufts of feathers around its neck resembling 16th-century neckwear.

Sandhill Cranes are so named after the low hills they congregate on during courtship displays.

The common name *Starling* is believed by some to come from the bird's shape in flight, when it looks like a little star.

THE BEST BIRDERS, though—"best" judged in moral terms, not by the size of life lists—are not merely observing machines; they also have a strict sense of honor: If they're not sure of the identification, it doesn't go down on the list. If the smallish bird on the branch betrays no sign of white wing bars, or if it

FROM THE VERB *TO BIRD*

BY PETER CASWELL

does not make the distinctive *pee-a-wee* call, or if it is wagging its tail, phoebe-like, it will not be recorded as an Eastern Pewee. For most official counts and contests, where accuracy and fair play are emphasized, an identification must be confirmed by a second person. When they're on their own, however, birders must weigh the hoped-for against the seen, with nothing to prevent them from padding out their lists except their own integrity. In the vast majority of birding situations, no one will be checking lists for consistency or administering random urine tests; there's no point. Sure, I could mark off a Kirtland's Warbler on my life list right now, but even if I had the call and the field marks memorized, even if I convincingly claimed that I'd been to the bird's northern Michigan breeding grounds, I'd

gain nothing from it. There are no Nike endorsements, no soft
drink commercials for birders; my amateur status will remain
unthreatened for eternity. I can therefore afford to demand
evidence when I see what appears to be an unusual bird, as much
as I want to believe it's a new one for the life list.

Want to test a birder's integrity? Check his daily count list
for *Empidonax* flycatchers. The National Geographic Society's
Field Guide to the Birds of North America describes the members of
this genus, accurately, as "the banc of birdwatchers." Even for
experts, these small flycatchers are damn near impossible to
distinguish from one another except by habitat, which may
be shared by several species, and by song, which you'll hear
only during breeding season. All are drab, the sort of neutral
beige-ish colors that L.L. Bean would call *taupe*, *mushroom*, or *dun*
fading to *off-white*, *oatmeal*, or *ecru* underneath, and all have the
same white eye-ring and two white wing bars. "Nondescript" is,
ironically, the perfect description of an *Empidonax*.

And what sort of person is obsessed with these birds?
Imagine a classical music lover who has a favorite composer—
Beethoven, let's say—and a favorite piece by that composer—let's
say the Third Symphony—and a favorite conductor—Herbert

Von Karajan with the Berlin Philharmonic—and imagine that this music lover will happily discuss with you the reasons why these are his favorites; that's the personality type of your average birder. But a birder whose expertise allows him to reliably identify the various birds of the *Empidonax* genus is like the music lover who owns *all* of the three or four different Karajan recordings of each individual Beethoven symphony and will hold forth for hours on which *version* is the best and why. It's impressive that he can do so, but there can't be very many people with whom he can talk about it. The *Empidonax* genus is a topic of similar narrowness.

So how will these paragons of dullness, these Babbitts with beaks, these tiny proles of the avian world help determine integrity? Easy. Over a period of years, an honest birder may be in a position to see any or all of the so-called "Empids," so five to ten different species may well appear on his *life* list. On a *daily* count, however, especially in the fall or winter, the odds of any but the most expert birder getting a firm ID on more than a couple of these species is slim to none. If such a count list says only "Empid—sp?" you can trust your life, your car, and your daughter to this person. If you see "Empid—(Acadian)," he'd better be from the Southeast, where the Acadian Flycatcher is the only breeding Empid; if not, the IRS probably wants to talk to him, though you as a private citizen can lend him books and expect to get them back eventually. If, however, you see a list from a daily count with an unbroken string of "Alder Flycatcher, Willow Flycatcher, Least Flycatcher," etc., beware! He may not swipe the silverware, but you can bet that he'll try to get you involved with Amway, or maybe put your name down to become part of his long-distance calling circle.

The way I figure, if you're going to lie about the birds you see, lie BIG. Why worry about fudging an indeterminate Empid into an Alder Flycatcher? Just go ahead and put down all the rarest birds: *Bachman's Warbler, Red-cocked Woodpecker, California Condor.* Go nuts! You don't even need to leave the house! Why not include species from other continents? *Peruvian Cock-of-the-Rock, Egyptian Vulture, Galapagos Penguin!* Come on! Who's going to stop you? Put down *extinct* birds! *Dodo! Heath Hen! Passenger Pigeon!* Hell, make up your *own* species! *Lesser Scottish Hamster-catcher! Parallel Parkingbird! Gabardine Trouser-thrush!* Oh, like anybody's going to check. Go ahead! Have fun!

Just don't say you're birding.

Birding the Internet

THE INTERNET offers everything from up-to-the-minute birding hotlines, live chat rooms, and message boards to sites that allow you to do virtual birding. When you can't be out in the field, sitting in front of your computer has become one of the best alternatives. Ask fellow birders questions, learn about migrations in your area, and test your ID skills on virtual tours that challenge the field birder with realistic sounds and imagery.

Americanbirding.org

You don't have to be a member of the American Birding Association to enjoy the group's extensive Web site, but membership does go a long way in bird habitat conservation. Joining the "Birders' Exchange" program helps the ABA toward its goal of providing neotropical areas with the basic equipment and educational materials needed to address migratory bird issues and conservation. The site also lists events, opportunities, and activities for young birders, and sells books, optics, and accessories.

Birdwatching-bliss.com

With the motto "A bad day of bird-watching is still better than a good day at work," Birdwatching-bliss.com is all about the happy birder. Far less technical than other popular birding sites, this is a forum for beginning and backyard birders. With great tips from squirrelproofing your feeder to creating a hummingbird habitat in your garden, this whimsical site is perfect for birders who want to bring the action right to their own backyard.

Cornell Lab of Ornithology (www.birds.cornell.edu)

Affiliated with Cornell University, the Web site of the Cornell Lab of Ornithology is a great resource for both researchers and what the lab calls "citizen scientists." With a very strong emphasis on conservation, the lab aims to get interested laypeople involved in monitoring bird populations with professional scientists. At-large lab projects involve counting birds you see in your area, and everyone who enjoys birds is encouraged to take part.

eBird.org

eBird.org provides a simple way for birders to keep track of the birds they see every day throughout the country. The site houses an extensive database where you can log your own bird observations and maintain lists of birds you've seen, as well as learn what other eBirders are reporting from across the country.

Fatbirder.com

Boasting a page for every country and state in the world, a page for every bird family, and tens of thousands of links about birding everywhere in the world, Fatbirder.com is full to bursting with information. Content on these pages is mostly written by faithful readers—the Web masters ask users to submit introductions to pages they know about, or submit photos for the "Bird of the Week." The site also contains up-to-the-minute ornithology news and articles as well as reviews of recently published field guides, audio guides, and DVDs.

Geobirds.com

After launching in January 2005, Geobirds.com has quickly become a reliable sounding board and reference for North American birders. Becoming a part of this online community is free and offers features such as an easy-to-use bird identification tool called the "BirdBrain."

The site also uses Google map technology for birders to share their sightings with fellow enthusiasts across the country.

Opticsblog.com

There seems to be a blogger for everything under the sun, so don't be surprised to find a binocular enthusiast who has a lot to say about the optics tools of the birding trade. Entries range from "Compact Binoculars I Have Loved" to "Telescopes for Christmas." This is your one-stop blog for everything you need to know before making any optics purchases. And if you benefit from the advice, go ahead and leave a comment using the comments feature available on every post.

WorldTwitch.com

For those interested in rare bird findings around the world, this is a site to bookmark! Updated frequently, WorldTwitch.com rounds up all the news in rare-bird findings in the Africa, Americas, Asia, Australia, and the Middle East. Search by region or country, and listen to birdsongs from around the world by following the extensive links available on the "Sounds" page.

Quail in Autumn
By William Jay Smith

Autumn has turned the dark trees toward the hill;
The wind has ceased; the air is white and chill.
Red leaves no longer dance against your foot,
The branch reverts to tree, the tree to root.

And now in this bare place your step will find
A twig that snaps flintlike against the mind;
Then thundering above your giddy head,
Small quail dart up, through shafting sunlight fled.

Like brightness buried by one's sullen mood
The quail rise startled from the threadbare wood;
A voice, a step, a swift sun-thrust of feather
And earth and air come properly together.

The Olive Oropendola is of course olive in color—except for its bright yellow tail feathers—and is known for making curious nests in its home in the Amazon Basin. Colonial breeders, oropendolas will set up camp in a tree with long woven basket nests suspended from the end of each branch.

The Greater Rhea has very large wings but does not use them—not to fly, anyway. To escape his predators, the Greater Rhea relies on his long, strong legs instead. And at more

Birds of South America

than 4 feet tall, he can make himself surprisingly invisible by lying flat in the grass with his legs straight out in front of him. You'll find him in open country from Brazil to central Argentina.

Fossil records show that Undulated Tinamous have been around for some 10 million years, living often very secluded and secret lives in the dark, dense forest lowlands of South America. For a bird that is grouselike in appearance, the eggs of the tinamou are particularly beautiful:

green, turquoise, purple, and wine red with a gloss similar to porcelain.

Proof that you really are what you eat: The Scarlet Ibis, which lives along the coastline from Venezuela to Brazil, is a striking scarlet red in color due to the carotene present in the crustaceans, fish, and algae it consumes.

King Vultures really live up to their name. These raptors circle savannas for dead meat; if they come upon a carcass that has already been discovered by other vultures, the rest will make way for the Kings, which are significantly superior in size and strength.

Cerro Acon...
...est point in S...

Found only along the coasts of Peru and Chile, the Inca Tern's most distinctive feature is its white plume feathers, which take the shape of a long, curling mustache above the beak in both male and female. Biologists have found that the condition of an Inca Tern's mustache is directly related to its physical health and reproductive performance.

The Red-fan Parrot is named for its incredible ability to fan the blue and red feathers around its head when excited—creating a huge, colorful crown. The bird is an important part of the Amazon Basin's ecology as a seed disperser.

The Hoatzin has a digestive system unique among birds—in fact, it's much closer to a cow's than a bird's! Hoatzins eat leaves and fruit, store them in their gut until the material ferments, and then feed on the fermented fodder. To see this fascinating bird, head to Venezuela, Bolivia, or Brazil.

The largest wren species in the world, the Black-capped Donacobius, is found from Panama to Argentina. These birds are known to sing together in pairs, each bird bobbing its head and wagging its tail.

Spanning all the way from Mexico to Argentina (and sometimes found in South Florida), the Bananaquit has an interesting name and interesting tendencies: Since it is unable to hover like a hummingbird in order to get pollen from the base of flowers, it performs entertaining acrobatic maneuvers.

The Rufous Motmot in the Amazon Basin is destined to be a slacker. While beautiful, it's a sluggish bird with small feet and a large bill that sits and waits for prey to appear in its vicinity.

The Andes region is home to the world's largest hummer—the aptly named Giant Hummingbird. Because of its size, its wingbeats are slower and more visible as it hovers, batlike, in front of a flower to take nectar.

The Rusty-belted Tapaculo is so named for its tail, which is always cocked up high. *Tapaculo* is Spanish for "cover your rear end." These birds show off their rear ends in the rain forest from western Brazil to Colombia, Ecuador, and Peru.

Native to rain forests and subtropical forests, the Royal Flycatcher is named for its impressive and vividly colored crest—which appears only very rarely, when the bird is in distress.

In this excerpt, a young Kenn Kaufman is nearing the end of his infamous record-breaking Big Year. He takes a break from his listing to join a Christmas Bird Count in Texas.

MORNING CAME TO THE A-FRAME as a chorus of rustlings and shufflings, as people crawled out of their sleeping bags in the dark and started off to reach their birding areas by first light. I lingered in the warm blankets a while—there was no point in looking for seabirds

FROM KINGBIRD HIGHWAY
BY KENN KAUFMAN

in the dark—but as soon as gray dawn lit the windows, I shoved my backpack into a corner and started off alone down the beach.

A gusty cold wind was blowing under a dark and restless sky. The pale sand beach was deserted except for a few Sanderlings, nervously skittering ahead of me. Behind the dunes the tawny beach grass whipped in the wind, and the wooden houses on stilts looked shuttered up and empty.

In the mile between the A-frame and the base of the jetty, as I was waking up more thoroughly, I began to notice just how loud the ocean was. The jumbled gray peaks of the waves turned to brown as they roiled up silt in the shallows, and then to white as they smashed on the beach. Big waves were visible as far out as I could see, all the way to where the gray ocean blended into gray sky; the lack of any stable horizon gave an unsettled feeling to the scene.

The Freeport jetty was a massive pile of stone blocks, incredibly long, extending perhaps half a mile out to sea. A similar jetty paralleled it a few hundred yards away; between the two ran the ship channel that led to the inner harbor. No boats seemed to be traversing the channel today.

Looking out along the jetty, I could see waves breaking violently out near the end. *Hot rats*, I thought; *it's no wonder they can't usually get anyone to go out there.* I was too unfamiliar with the area to realize just how much the weather had worsened since the afternoon before. *Well, this is the West*, I said to myself; *I'm not going to chicken out on my assignment.* There was no point in hesitating. The big gray slabs of stone that formed the center of the jetty were almost level, and I started out toward the end, leaping from rock to rock, in a hurry now to get out there and man my post.

Out at the very tip of the jetty, I found a solid place to station myself, a huge level block of stone. Planting the tripod firmly on the rock, I aimed Edgar Kincaid's telescope out to sea. I was determined that no seabird would slip past me unnoticed. Alternating between

scanning with binoculars and sweeping the distant waves with the telescope, I began my day's vigil.

It was good to be just birding, just looking to see what was there, not trying to build any personal list. At the precount gathering the night before, so many people had been asking, "Could you get any new year birds tomorrow?" "Do you think you'll win the Big Year competition?" It was impossible to explain to them that I really did not care anymore.

The Big Year had been a great excuse to go birding. To both Floyd Murdoch and me, that had mattered more than the numerical outcome. All along, Floyd had been more interested in the protection of birds and their habits than in the accumulation of checkmarks. As for me, my own passion for list-chasing was dwindling fast, while my interest in the birds themselves was becoming stronger than ever. So the contest was coming to matter least of all to the contestants.

The whistling wind that flapped my poncho around also drove each breaker against the base of the jetty at my feet. The waves seemed to be getting bigger. I was being misted with spray from every wave now, and some of them broke high enough that water

washed around the soles of my beat-up hiking boots. As a whimsical precaution, I tied the drawstring of my poncho to the tripod that held the borrowed telescope.

Gulls were tacking into the wind, hanging on updrafts where the gusts were deflected by the jetty, streaking downwind on backswept wings like errant boomerangs. They were wonderful to watch, but did I really know them? All the North American species of gulls were on my list, so I should have recognized each one here with confidence. But I didn't. Not really. In the past I had always checked them off by finding the adults in their distinctive plumages, ignoring most of the motley younger birds. So, what were all these young gulls flying past now? I thought they were probably all Ring-bills and Herring Gulls; but if something rare had been among them, I would not have recognized it. I still had a lot to learn.

One thing was becoming obvious to me now: list-chasing was not the best way to learn birds. It had been a good way to start, an incentive for getting to a lot of places and seeing a lot of species. But the lure of running up a big list made it all too tempting to simply check off a bird and run on to the next, without taking time to really get to know them. And there was so much that I did not know.

210

So much left to learn . . . And one other lesson was sinking in, near the end of 1973, as I ran into the expectations of other birders. Just because I had broken listing records, they expected me to be a top-notch birder—and I was not. They were comparing me to Ted Parker, who had set the record just two years before—but there was really no comparison. None of us realized then just how fast the world of bird listing had been changing. Indeed, the entire approach to doing a Big Year had been undergoing a radical change.

Ted Parker had set his record in 1971 on the strength of sheer skill and knowledge and energy. For me, as for Floyd Murdoch, the mix had involved less skill and a lot more information: just two years had made that much difference, as the fledgling American Birding Association had broadcast the directions to dozens of good sites for scarce birds. The totals amassed by Murdoch and me would be edged out in 1976, as a young ornithology student named Scott Robinson made a low-budget, high-knowledge run around the continent. But that would be the last time that any record could be set by a birder who focused on the normally occurring birds.

The information explosion, in birding as in everything else, was bringing us more and more data, faster and faster. The new bird-

finding booklets let us know about good birding spots that had been productive within the last five or ten years. The notes and inserts in *Birding* gave us specific sites that had been productive within the last year or so, even within the last few months. But before long, the burgeoning communication among birders would bring news of rarities that were *really* current: found today, even found within the last few hours.

A couple of times in 1973 I had heard about rare visitors in time to go and look for them, like the Loggerhead Kingbird that had spent the whole winter in Florida. But before the end of the 1970s, the growth of birding "hotlines" would make it possible for birders to find out about such strays almost instantly. A birder with money could then jump on the next flight, rent a car, and check off a bird that he had never even heard of just a few hours earlier. It was inevitable that Big Year listing would come to focus more and more on such rarities. Listing would shift away from knowledge and planning and experience, toward contacts and hotlines and money.

And, no doubt, it would continue to be a tremendous amount of fun for those who could afford it, the greatest of games. But list-chasing had lost most of its appeal for me. What I needed to do now was to go back and look at all those birds again, taking more time.

By now the sea was in a frenzy all around my perch near the end of the jetty. The waves were still coming from ahead and to my right. I could not see them approaching as individual waves, only as a dance of whitecaps, but I could tell each time one arrived, running *wham!* into the massive rocks and sending up a curtain of spray. If I looked quickly back along the jetty I could see how the angle of the breaker would run itself out against the line of rocks, and at the same time I would feel the water from the spent wave washing over my feet. Gradually it was coming to me that this must be unusual weather, and that perhaps I should move back a little from the end of the jetty. But I would take one more scan out over the ocean first.

Gulls had been flying past the jetty and out over the whitecaps, but scanning farther out I suddenly picked up one that looked different. With a start, I realized it was a species I could recognize with certainty, one I'd seen by the thousands in Alaska: a Black-legged Kittiwake, a rare bird in Texas, the kind of prize that Victor had hoped would come out of my vigil on the jetty. I strained to follow it in the telescope as the wind rocked me and spray stung my eyes.

Seeing the kittiwake brought back sudden images of Gambell, Alaska, the magical place that I had visited half a year and most of a continent earlier. Perhaps my Big Year attempt had no value

213

in itself, but it had led me to incredible places, a whole series of extraordinary destinations. It had taken me through life-changing experiences. Regardless of final list totals, it had been worthwhile.

Listing, at its best, could be a wonderful quest, I reflected. We list-chasing birders, at our best, could be like knights seeking the Holy Grail—except that the birds were real, and we birders were rewarded at every turn. If we made an honest effort, the birds would come. This kittiwake, appearing out of the storm like a winged messenger, seemed to confirm that. Inspired, I began another scan of the ocean.

Just then I felt another wave washing over my feet, tugging at my ankles. The breakers were obviously getting higher. Despite all my macho intentions, common sense was insisting that I really should move back a little. But at that moment, I picked up something flying far out over the horizon. A dark gull, flapping hard—No! it was a jaeger, another bird that would be a great addition to the count. But which kind? With difficulty I found it in the telescope and struggled to see field marks. White flashes at the bend of the wing, dark chest band; could be either Pomarine or Parasitic. Salt stung my eyes and I lost the bird, still undecided about which it was. But maybe I could find it again. I would take one more scan—

214

FROM KINGBIRD HIGHWAY

The next wave rumbled up onto the jetty, and I could feel that this would be a big one. Instinctively I flexed my knees to brace against the current, but it was futile. With a sense of unreality I felt my feet slipping, and then I was sliding sideways, flailing for the telescope, tumbling off the top of the jetty. My shoulder hit a rock with a tooth-rattling crunch, and then I was gulping salt water and thrashing in the cold green darkness.

When I came to the surface I was looking up at the jetty, now seeming to tower above me, several yards away. My tattered jeans and boots were heavy as lead, and my poncho wrapped around my arms like a shroud, but when I reached for the poncho drawstring that had been tied to the tripod and scope I felt nothing—the cord had pulled free, and the telescope was gone.

Another wave crashed over the top of the jetty, and I was underwater again. Floundering toward the boulders at the jetty's base, I grabbed them and pulled myself up. The rocks were covered with barnacles, and their razor edges sliced my palms. Surprised, I loosened my grip, and another wave knocked me off again.

Treading water heavily, I tried to think rationally about what to do. The sharp little cones of barnacles appeared to cover every inch of the jetty rocks near water level. For a moment I considered trying to swim to shore, but the beach was so far away; I doubted I could swim that far in my sodden clothes. I had to go up the rocks to survive.

Twice more I tried to climb the rough boulders. Twice more, waves coming over the top of the jetty knocked me loose, sending me sliding down, barnacles ripping my palms and the knees of my jeans. But finally I was able to clamber up to the top of the jetty, above the level of the barnacles. Slowly, half crouching and half crawling, clinging to the rough rocks when each wave broke, I made my way back toward shore. It seemed like an eternity before I was finally standing on the beach again.

My hands were bleeding and stinging so badly that I could not even hold my binoculars. There was no point in looking for assistance at the deserted houses behind the line of dunes. Then I remembered the Shrimp Hut, up the beach near the A-frame, where the group had had dinner the night before. Maybe it was open today. Shivering now in the cold wind, I walked back in that direction.

The waitresses in the Shrimp Hut were shocked by my appearance—and no wonder. As unkempt as I usually looked, I was now also sopping wet, bleeding, and probably wild-eyed. But when they saw my hands, their expressions changed. Although the

216

waitresses were no older than I, their maternal instincts seemed to take over. They sat me down, washed and soaked and bandaged my hands, and even spoon-fed me some warm soup. Silently I rebuked myself for having laughed at their mock sailor uniforms the night before; regardless of their uniforms, they looked like angels to me now.

I tried to pay for the bandages and the soup, but they refused the wet dollar bills I fished out of my wallet. So I thanked them again and turned to leave.

"You're not going back out on the jetty, are you?"

"I have to," I said. "This is our big bird count."

Trudging back up the beach, I hardly noticed that the waves still pounded the sand, the wind still gusted and cried; I was inured to the weather. Once again I picked my way out onto the jetty, jumping from rock to rock, gauging how far I could go in safety. A little more than halfway out, just before the first stretch where the waves began to get bad, I took my stand.

You're not going back out there, are you? But of course I was. It was the only thing to do. The certainty of that decision gave me a sense of calm. In the midst of the turbulent sea and sky, I was overcome by a great feeling of peace: I was doing exactly what I was meant to do today. *Any day could be a special day, and you just had to get outside, and see what the birds were doing* . . . Birding is what I came here for; this is how I spend this day and my days and my life.

The borrowed telescope was gone, my hands were bandaged, and my cheap binoculars were clouded with salt water, but I was keeping my vigil. I could still see rare seabirds if they came in close. As the afternoon waned, the sun might find a break in the clouds, and then it would be low in the western sky behind me—flooding everything in front of me with perfect light.

Somewhere out there, maybe not too far away, jaegers were coursing over the waves. They might come this way again. I was sure they would. Experience had shown me that jaegers and other seabirds might come in closer to shore early in the morning and then again late in the afternoon and evening. Surely in this stormy weather they would come in close. I would be here, ready, when they came.

THE SEA-GULL

By Ogden Nash

Hark to the whimper of the sea-gull;
He weeps because he's not an ea-gull.
Suppose you were, you silly sea-gull,
Could you explain it to your she-gull?

220

Get Connected!

YOU MAY THINK there is nothing better than heading out on a solo hike to seek bird sightings in peace. And while this is essential to the experience of any good birder, there are also many advantages to birding in groups. This is especially true for beginners, who may find that others in the group—with their more practiced eyes—are able to identify birds quickly and accurately. Let these people be your guide, or join up to make friends who share your unique passion.

Birding clubs and organizations are vast and varied. Read on for information about finding the best local knowledge, resources for further education in birding and conservation, and tips for becoming a social birder.

National Organizations

National Audubon Society (www.audubon.org). Founded in 1905, the society now has more than 500 chapters across the country that organize both birding excursions and environmental conservation efforts. Membership benefits include subscription to the bimonthly publication *Audubon*, invitations to birding events and travel packages, and special offers on merchandise. Visit the Web site to find your local chapter.

American Birding Association (www.americanbirding.org). Founded in 1969, ABA prints multiple publications, maintains a membership directory, and organizes national conferences and conventions.

Membership benefits include subscription to the bimonthly *Birding* and the newsletter *Winging It*, along with a membership directory. The Web site includes activities listings for your area.

Independent Organizations

While the national organizations have branches in every state, some states have their own independent birding societies, which usually date back to the 1900s or even earlier. Often geared toward a certain general interest—a specific species of bird, a particular local conservation effort—these state offices are great resources for both beginning and seasoned birders.

Observatories and Laboratories

Observatories and laboratories offer a great opportunity for birders of all ages. Publicly funded and stocked both with experts in the field and excellent conditions for birding on site, these organizations are a great way for bird enthusiasts to follow their passion as well as help conserve biological diversity. Education in conservation, ornithology, and biology is offered at the Cornell Laboratory of Ornithology (www.birds.cornell.edu) and the Point Reyes Bird Observatory in California (www.prbo.org), among many other such excellent institutions across the country.

More Tips for Social Birding

- Check the yellow pages for listings of outfitters, pet stores, and other retailers in your area that stock birding materials and equipment. Owners and employees will likely have connections to local birding groups.

- Look for birding or field ornithology classes in the course listings of your local community college, high school, museum, or zoo. The leaders of these programs can likely introduce you to their birding networks.

- Contact your local paper for the columnist who specializes in nature and the outdoors. He or she is likely to be in touch with local birders and privy to their events, trips, and meeting dates.

- If all else fails, begin a group of your own. By posting local ads, you're sure to fish out birders who would be grateful for your company!

Wild Geese

By Elinor Chipp

I heard the wild geese flying
  In the dead of the night,
With beat of wings and crying
  I heard the wild geese flying.

And dreams in my heart sighing
  Followed their northward flight.
I heard the wild geese flying
  In the dead of the night.

Once listed in the *Guinness Book of World Records* as "the world's most dangerous bird," the Southern Cassowary is a flightless avian with many defensive weapons at its disposal. It has a bony casque on the top of its head, which allows it to run quickly (32 mph) through dense vegetation. Its strong legs can deliver quite a kick, and it has a bladelike outer toe that should not be trifled with.

Birds of Oceania

The largest Australian bird is the Emu, which has lived on the continent for at least 80 million years.

The national bird of New Zealand is actually difficult to find. The forest-dwelling Brown Kiwi hides during the daytime hours and feeds at night using its excellent sense of smell—perhaps aided by the fact that its nostrils are at the tip of the bill.

The unusual Magpie-Goose inhabits only northern Australia and southern New Guinea. The sole member of its bird family, the Magpie-Goose has only partially webbed feet and—unlike other geese—has no flightless period.

Mallefowl are large, ground-dwelling birds from southern Australia known for their egg-incubation system. After digging a hole and filling it with twigs and leaves, the male waits for rain to moisten the nest, and then fills it with soil. Throughout the incubation process, the male is often seen opening and rotating the contents of the nest to control the heat of the plant material.

Not all pigeons are gray city-dwellers like the ones you see in London and New York City. New Guinea boasts the beautiful Victoria Crowned Pigeon, which has a rich blue coloring and a fan-shaped tufted crest that is permanently raised, giving it a royal air.

What looks like rainbow sherbet and has a whooping call? A male Superb Fruit-dove, which dwells in the rain forest throughout Oceania.

Parrots abound in this region, ranging from the colorful Eastern Rosella and Turquoise Parrot, to the talkative Gray Parrot, to the bare-faced Vulture Parrot. There is even a small population of Kakapo, nocturnal, flightless parrots that creep through established forest paths at night looking for food.

A few beautiful cockatoos live in Oceania, including the western-endemic Short-billed Black-cockatoo and the Sulfur-crested Cockatoo, which has a crest that looks like a yellow flower blossoming from the top of its head.

Look hard and you might be able to spot a Papuan Frogmouth, a nocturnal bird that camouflages itself in the day by looking like a dead tree branch. At night, it searches out prey from its perch, and then swoops down to capture food in its open mouth.

Finally, a bird even your kitty will like—or at least like the looks of, as New Guinea's Feline Owlet-nightjar's long, sensitive whiskers make it look a bit catlike.

Hands-down the best name? Laughing Kookaburra. Say that without cracking a smile! The largest of the kingfishers lives in eastern and southwestern Australia, often staying with its parents after it becomes an adult to help out and guard the family territory with cackling calls.

Some of the most stunning and colorful shows of feathers are found among birds-of-paradise.

New Guinea hosts the King Bird-of-paradise, with a coiled feather vance; the spectacular flank feathers of the Lesser Bird-of-paradise; and the male Blue Bird-of-paradise, which boasts 13.5-inch tail streamers.

The male Superb Lyrebird of Australia puts on a fantastic courtship display that involves mimicry, dancing, and vibrating his tail while standing on a mound of damp soil, which he scrapes together just for the occasion.

Splendid Fairy-wrens, as well as most other fairy-wrens in Australia, live and breed in small groups working together to feed and prepare their young for the world. Communities of 5.5-inch-long Splendid Fairy-wrens feature one bright blue male amid the dull-colored females.

Kenn Kaufman

KENN KAUFMAN was born in 1954 in South Bend, Indiana. Legendary for his work in modern ornithology, birdwatching, conservation, and field guides, Kaufman began his studies when he was just seven years old. That was the year he found his first field guide in a library. He'd already developed a keen interest in the birds he saw every day in South Bend, and this book helped him dig deeper—he even began distinguishing between starlings and grackles at his young age.

Nine years later, Kaufman dropped out of high school and began hitchhiking across the United States, Canada, and Mexico, traveling about 80,000 miles in one year, crisscrossing the continent to see as many different birds as he could. At 19 he set the Big Year record for the most North American bird species sighted in one year: 666 in total. His notoriety led to a job as a leader of international birding tours for Wings Inc. and Victor Emanuel Nature Tours.

The National Audubon Society asked him to become associate editor for the magazine *American Birds*, a somewhat

technical publication for serious birdwatchers. Kaufman then received a contract to write and illustrate his own field guide for the trusted and renowned Peterson Field Guide series. He published *A Field Guide to Advanced Birding* in 1990. In 1992, he received the Ludlow Griscom Distinguished Birder Award, the highest honor awarded by the American Birding Association.

It was around this time that Kaufman started to notice aspects of the birding world that didn't make sense to him. Surrounded by serious birders who were very passionate about what they did—to the point of engaging in long arguments about molt sequences—Kaufman realized that serious birders seemed to have lost sight of the fact that bird habitats were becoming increasingly endangered all around them. Alarmed by the drastic need for conservation, he knew he would have to reach outside the small circle of serious birders if he wanted to make changes in environmental policy.

Kaufman aimed to attract beginning birders and more casual observers in his next field guide, which featured photos that were digitally edited for accuracy and direct comparability, making their subjects more easily identifiable to the average birder. Kaufman felt that if he could get more of the general public to identify birds in their day-to-day lives, those individuals would become more open to conservation efforts for birds and other wildlife.

Since then, Kaufman has gone on to publish *Lives of North American Birds*, *Kaufman Focus Guides: Birds of North America*, and a now classic memoir about his teenage Big Year experience, *Kingbird Highway*.

Kenn Kaufman is currently the field editor for *Audubon* magazine, published by the National Audubon Society. He also writes for various other sources and works mostly on a freelance basis in his many efforts to bring about more awareness of bird habitat conservation.

A Little Bird Told Me...
A Birdsong Q & A

Q. How do birds know how to sing?

A. Birdsong develops in two different ways among species. Many birds are born with their particular birdsongs encoded in their DNA, and those songs do not alter over time despite the influence of other birds around them. Birds that were born to sing—their own way—include loons, ducks, geese, shorebirds, gulls, pigeons, doves, owls, and woodpeckers.

While most birds hatch with the innate knowledge of a general outline of their own birdsong, many are able to learn songs and sounds from other birds. The mockingbird is the most famous of this type, and is named for its well-known reputation for mimicking the sounds of other songbirds.

The European Starling is another mimicker—in fact, one of the most incredible: His extremely long songs incorporate many of the sounds he hears from his neighbors strung together to create a unique and often improvised birdsong.

Q. Why do some birds learn new songs while others do not?

A. Scientists are still trying to figure this out, but there are a few theories and tantalizing facts out there:

- Learning birdsong from a neighboring bird may help facilitate communication among birds coexisting in certain areas.
- Some think that the shared birdsong can even create a community effect among differing species, so that birds

234

CAROL PRACTICE.

Q. Do southern birds have a drawl?

A. Just like your cousin from Nashville and our friendly neighbors to the north, birds have their own dialects, or accents, depending on where they live. These dialects can vary greatly among regions of the United States— even among towns. For instance, ornithologists studying Martha's Vineyard have found that dialects among the chickadees vary greatly over the tiny 100-square-mile island.

can work together to defend shared territories.

 Sharing and learning the songs of those around them could also be a way for males to impress females by showing that they know the local vocabulary and are thus successful and stable mates.

It has been found that via the process of evolution, some species have in relatively recent times either lost or gained the ability to learn birdsong from others.

Q. Why do I typically only hear males singing?

A. The lilting, graceful birdsong you hear each spring is coming almost exclusively from male birds. Female birds largely do not take part because they are not courting their mates. In studies of the motivation behind male birdsong, researchers have found that in most species all that warbling is done for the ladies. In fact, a study of the Chestnut-sided Warbler revealed

that when a female is placed in his territory, he is largely silent. Once she is taken away, however, he sings six or seven songs per minute until she returns.

Even though females rarely sing like their male counterparts, female birds aren't always quiet. Some, such as the White-crowned Sparrow, speak up occasionally, while others like blackbirds are more frequently vocal. Among blackbirds, the female Red-winged often answers her mate when he sings, although her response is decidedly less musical. Male and female grackles often perch together in early spring and seem to answer each other back and forth, with the female again producing a raspier, less musical sound.

Q. When is the best time to hear birdsong?

A. Birdsong is at its most intense at dawn's first light. This is the best time to hear your favorite songbird spice up his routine a little. While it's still an enigma as to why songbirds sing so intensely at dawn, everyone agrees that the phenomenon is worth getting up for.

Theodore A. Parker III

THEODORE (TED) A. PARKER III, an American
ornithologist who possessed a remarkable ear for
recognizing bird sounds, was born on April 1, 1953.
He grew up in Lancaster, Pennsylvania, in a family that
supported his passion for natural history. Even as a teen,
Parker demonstrated an extraordinary ability to identify
birds and other wildlife.

During his last semester of high school, Parker began
his Big Year, a competition to see as many species of birds
as possible in 365 days. Traveling along the Atlantic coast
near his Lancaster home, Parker was able to see huge
numbers of birds. That fall he enrolled at the University
of Arizona, allowing him to add southwestern and Pacific
avians to his list. At the end of 1971, Parker broke the
standing North American Big Year record by viewing 626
species. He instantly became an icon for young birders all
over the country.

241

During his college years, Parker took his first ornithological expedition to South America, one that would lead to a lifelong passion for neotropical birds and the protection of their habitats. In Baton Rouge, he supported himself by leading birding tours for Victor Emanuel Nature Tours, which allowed him to continue developing his skills in the field, much to the delight of all who traveled with him. Parker possessed an innate gift for recognizing bird vocalizations and behavioral patterns, two very important factors in identifying birds in South America's dense neotropical forests. His repertoire consisted of over 2,000 bird vocalizations in the Andes and Amazon; moreover, each species usually has at least three different dialects. Parker would lead members of his tours deep into the wild and lure flocks by playing tape recordings of their sounds. He would then position the birders so they were out of the way but still able to easily view the flock.

Parker's abilities have become almost legendary among birdwatchers. If other ornithologists played him a tape of an unknown bird, he could always identify it—and could usually recognize other species in the background as well, not to mention the location of where the tape had been made. He could identify birdsongs even amid a cacophony of other forest noises, and he was able to single out a birdcall even if it was a member of a mixed-species flock. On one occasion, Parker was recording a chorus of birds in Bolivia when he realized that one of the birds was a previously unknown species of the antwren genus *Herpsilochmus*.

Parker is perhaps best known for two lasting contributions to world of ornithology. First is his archive of over 10,000 bird recordings, the world's largest collection, which is held at the Library of Natural Sounds at the Cornell Laboratory of Ornithology. And second is his role in the creation of the Rapid Assessment Program (RAP), which sends out international teams of tropical field biologists who can quickly provide the biological information needed to push for immediate conservation action and improve biodiversity protection. Parker was doing a survey for RAP in 1993 when he was tragically killed in a plane crash in western Ecuador along with three others. In his 40 years, Parker developed a reputation as one the best field ornithologists the world had ever known, in the process becoming a catalyst for conservation activism.

THE WATERFALLS OF THE SIERRA ARE FREQUENTED BY ONLY ONE BIRD—THE OUZEL OR WATER THRUSH (*Cinclus Mexicanus, Sw.*) He is a singularly joyous and lovable little fellow, about the size of a robin,

FROM # THE AMERICAN DIPPER

BY JOHN MUIR

clad in a plain waterproof suit of bluish gray, with a tinge of chocolate on the head and shoulders. In form he is about as smoothly plump and compact as a pebble that has been whirled in a pot-hole, the flowing contour of his body being interrupted only by his strong feet and bill, the crisp wing-tips, and the up-slanted wren-like tail.

Among all the countless waterfalls I have met in the course of ten years' exploration in the

244

FROM THE AMERICAN DIPPER

Sierra, whether among the icy peaks, or warm foothills, or in the profound yosemitic cañons of the middle region, not one was found without its Ouzel. No cañon is too cold for this little bird, none too lonely, provided it be rich in falling water. Find a fall, or cascade, or rushing rapid, anywhere upon a clear stream, and there you will surely find its complementary Ouzel, flitting about in the spray, diving in foaming eddies, whirling like a leaf among beaten foam-bells; ever vigorous and enthusiastic, yet self-contained, and neither seeking nor shunning your company.

If disturbed while dipping about in the margin shallows, he either sets off with a rapid whir to some other feeding-ground up or down the stream, or alights on some half-submerged rock or snag out in the current, and immediately begins to nod and courtesy like a wren, turning his head from side to side with many other odd dainty movements that never fail to fix the attention of the observer.

He is the mountain streams' own darling, the humming-bird of blooming waters, loving rocky ripple-slopes and sheets of foam as a bee loves flowers, as a lark loves sunshine and meadows. Among all the mountain birds, none has cheered me so much in my lonely wanderings—none so unfailingly. For both in winter and

summer he sings, sweetly, cheerily, independent alike of sunshine and of love, requiring no other inspiration than the stream on which he dwells. While water sings, so must he, in heat or cold, calm or storm, ever attuning his voice in sure accord; low in the drought of summer and the drought of winter, but never silent.

During the golden days of Indian summer, after most of the snow has been melted, and the mountain streams have become feeble—a succession of silent pools, linked together by shallow, transparent currents and strips of silvery lacework—then the song of the Ouzel is at its lowest ebb. But as soon as the winter clouds have bloomed, and the mountain treasuries are once more replenished with snow, the voices of the streams and ouzels increase in strength and richness until the flood season of early summer. Then the torrents chant their noblest anthems, and then is the flood-time of our songster's melody. As for weather, dark days and sun days are the same to him. The voices of most songbirds, however joyous, suffer a long winter eclipse; but the Ouzel sings on through all the seasons and every kind of storm. Indeed no storm can be more violent than those of the waterfalls in the midst of which he delights to dwell. However dark and boisterous the weather, snowing, blowing, or cloudy, all the same he sings, and with never a note of sadness. No need of spring sunshine to thaw *his* song, for it never freezes. Never shall you hear anything wintry from *his* warm breast; no pinched cheeping, no wavering notes between sorrow and joy; his mellow, fluty voice is ever tuned to downright gladness, as free from dejection as cock-crowing.

It is pitiful to see wee frost-pinched sparrows on cold mornings in the mountain groves shaking the snow from their feathers, and hopping about as if anxious to be cheery, then hastening back to their hidings out of the wind, puffing out their breast-feathers over their toes, and subsiding among the leaves, cold and breakfastless, while the snow continues to fall, and there is no sign of clearing. But the Ouzel never calls forth a single touch of pity; not because he is strong to endure, but rather because he seems to live a charmed life beyond the reach of every influence that makes endurance necessary.

One wild winter morning, when Yosemite Valley was swept its length from west to east by a cordial snow-storm, I sallied forth to see what I might learn and enjoy. A sort of gray, gloaming-like darkness filled the valley, the huge walls were out of sight, all ordinary sounds were smothered, and even the loudest booming of the falls was at times buried beneath the roar of the heavy-

laden blast. The loose snow was already over five feet deep on the meadows, making extended walks impossible without the aid of snowshoes. I found no great difficulty, however, in making my way to a certain ripple on the river where one of my Ouzels lived. He was at home, busily gleaning his breakfast among the pebbles of a shallow portion of the margin, apparently unaware of anything extraordinary in the weather. Presently he flew out to a stone against which the icy current was beating, and turning his back to the wind, sang as delightfully as a lark in springtime.

After spending an hour or two with my favorite, I made my way across the valley, boring and wallowing through the drifts, to learn as definitely as possible how the other birds were spending their time. The Yosemite birds are easily found during the winter because all of them excepting the Ouzel are restricted to the sunny north side of the valley, the south side being constantly eclipsed by the great frosty shadow of the wall. And because the Indian Cañon groves, from their peculiar exposure, are the warmest, the birds congregate there, more especially in severe weather.

I found most of the robins cowering on the lee side of the larger branches where the snow could not fall upon them, while two or three of the more enterprising were making desperate efforts to reach the mistletoe berries by clinging nervously to the under side of the snow-crowned masses, back downward, like woodpeckers. Every now and then they would dislodge some of the loose fringes of the snow-crown, which would come sifting down on them and send them screaming back to camp, where they would subside among their companions with a shiver, muttering in low, querulous chatter like hungry children.

Some of the sparrows were busy at the feet of the larger trees gleaning seeds and benumbed insects, joined now and then by a robin weary of his unsuccessful attempts upon the snow-covered berries. The brave woodpeckers were clinging to the snowless sides of the larger boles and overarching branches of the camp trees, making short flights from side to side of the grove, pecking now and then at the acorns they had stored in the bark, and chattering aimlessly as if unable to keep still, yet evidently putting in the time in a very dull way, like storm-bound travelers at a country tavern. The hardy nut-hatches were threading the open furrows of the trunks in their usual industrious manner, and

uttering their quaint notes, evidently less distressed than their neighbors. The Steller jays were of course making more noisy stir than all the other birds combined; ever coming and going with loud bluster, screaming as if each had a lump of melting sludge in his throat, and taking good care to improve the favorable opportunity afforded by the storm to steal from the acorn stores of the woodpeckers. I also noticed one solitary gray eagle braving the storm on the top of a tall pine-stump just outside the main grove. He was standing bolt upright with his back to the wind, a tuft of snow piled on his square shoulders, a monument of passive endurance. Thus every snow-bound bird seemed more or less uncomfortable if not in positive distress. The storm was reflected in every gesture, and not one cheerful note, not to say song, came from a single bill; their cowering, joyless endurance offering a striking contrast to the spontaneous, irrepressible gladness of the Ouzel, who could no more help exhaling sweet song then a rose sweet fragrance. He *must* sing though the heavens fall.

Even as the dying year approaches its end, there are bird voices to remind us that we have passed the winter solstice, and that already the days are lengthening toward spring.

ROBERT CUNNINGHAM MILLER

FESTIVALS OF FALL AND WINTER

Just because it's cold where you are doesn't mean it isn't a pleasant 70 degrees somewhere else! So pack up your tank top and shorts and head out to one of these festivals—all perfect excuses to get away for a weekend and observe birds you typically might not have a chance to see during the snowy months. If you already winter somewhere warm, head north to take in major bird events like the Fall Bald Eagle Festival in Alaska.

September

Hummer/Bird Celebration
Rockport, TX

This is one of the biggest festivals in the United States, with talks and events on all things hummingbird, from identification, banding, and photographing to field trips. You can also take in programs on butterflies, shorebirds, and backyard birdwatching.

Kern Valley Turkey Vulture Festival
Weldon, CA

Visit the southern Sierra's Kern River Valley to experience one of the largest-known Turkey Vulture migrations in the United States or Canada, as well as the height of fall land bird migration at desert oases. Join in the Turkey Vulture count and learn about geology, botany, moths, and reptiles.

October

Eastern Shore Birding Festival
Kiptopeke, VA

An annual celebration of the migrating neotropical songbirds and raptors on Virginia's eastern shore. Activities in the past have included lessons in songbird banding, a "schooner serenity" cruise, and trips to the Kiptopeke Hawk Observatory.

Cape May Autumn Festival/Bird Show
Cape May, NJ

Late October at Cape May along the Atlantic Flyway is a busy time for birders. This is when the greatest numbers of hawks, falcons, and other raptors pass by; when seabirds are at their most diverse; and when songbirds migrate through in the hundreds of thousands.

November

Wings Over Water
Outer Banks, NC

For more than 10 years, Wings Over Water has been considered the premier birding and nature festival on the Outer Banks. It offers 100 birding, paddling, and natural history excursions for avian enthusiasts.

Alaska Bald Eagle Festival
Haines, AK

Enjoy birding near the largest gathering of eagles in the world—more than 3,000—as they feed on a late run of salmon along a 4-mile stretch of the Chilkat River north of Haines each fall.

Festival of the Cranes
Soccoro, NM

The Bosque del Apache Wildlife Refuge celebrates the arrival of wintering Snow Geese and Sandhill Cranes in the hundreds of thousands.

Rio Grande Valley Birding Festival
Harlington, TX

With keynote speakers, a trade show, and seminars, this festival covers a bit of everything—and the field trips do, too. Take a day trip to bird at South Padre Island, explore the Upper Rio Grande, or search out local parrots with an expert guide!

December

YUCATÁN BIRD FESTIVAL
MEXICO

Take in Mayan ruins, 16th-century haciendas and towns, and a coastal reserve full of avians. The region offers 543 bird species, of which 16 are endemic and quasi-endemics.

January

MORRO BAY WINTER FESTIVAL
MORRO BAY, CA

Spend Martin Luther King Jr. weekend in sunny California by visiting this Globally Important Bird Area. Join a group for a Big Day or—for a less hectic morning—take a beginning kayak trip to see the Great Blue Heron nesting site.

ST. GEORGE WINTER FESTIVAL
ST. GEORGE, UT

Revel in the gorgeous sandstone cliffs and lava flows that surround St. George as local guides take you to nine of Washington County's birding hot spots searching for Red-napped Sapsuckers and Bald Eagles.

February

WINTER WINGS FESTIVAL
KLAMATH FALLS, OREGON

It's worth a trip to Klamath Basin just to witness the largest concentration of wintering Bald Eagles in the lower 48 states—but don't miss out on the rest of what this festival has to offer! Take a hot-air balloon ride, breakfast with Bald Eagles, spend the afternoon ice-skating, and view the beautiful local waterfowl.

Egrets
By Mary Oliver

Where the path closed
   down and over,
      through the scumbled leaves,
      fallen branches,
through the knotted catbrier,
   I kept going. Finally
    I could not
     save my arms
       from the thorns; soon
the mosquitoes
  smelled me, hot
    and wounded, and came
      wheeling and whining.
       And that's how I came

to the edge of the pond:
    black and empty
        except for a spindle
        of bleached reeds
at the far shore
    which, as I looked,
        wrinkled suddenly
            into three egrets—
a shower
    of white fire!
        Even half-asleep they had
            such faith in the world
that had made them—
    tilting through the water,
        unruffled, sure,
            by the laws
of their faith not logic,
    they opened their wings
        softly and stepped
            over every dark thing.

- Arizona's Cave Creek Canyon is the best spot in the United States to see Elegant Trogons. Other highlights are the Mexican Jay, several species of owls, and the Montezuma Quail.

- Ramsey Canyon Preserve in Arizona is the spot to see hummingbirds. In fall this area bustles with 10 different species, including Magnificent, Broad-tailed, and Black-chinned Hummingbirds.

Birding in the West

- Situated in the Mojave Desert, the Red Rock Canyon Nature Conservation Area offers birders a 13-mile winding loop to enjoy the scenery from the air-conditioned comfort of their cars. Along with Golden Eagles, Red-tailed Hawks, Greater Roadrunners, and Cactus Wrens, visitors can see forest birds as they migrate through the desert to their western summer homes.

- One hundred sixty springs flow into the Ruby Lake National Wildlife Refuge in Nevada's Great Basin. These springs provide a perfect habitat to see more than 200 pairs of White-faced Ibises, Canvasback Ducks, and Trumpeter Swans, whose booming calls echo off the mountains after dark.

- While in New Mexico, don't miss the Bosque del Apache National Wildlife Refuge. With more than 12,000 cranes, 25,000 geese, and 40,000 ducks all wintering there, the reserve is crawling with birders as well as eagles, wild turkeys, and Blue Grosbeaks.

- If you feel like getting some space, head to Denali National Park and Preserve, which spans 6 million acres in Alaska. Take it all (or at least some of it) in by bus or backpack, looking for the Arctic Terns that travel 22,000 miles every year from Antarctica, as well as such northern specialties as the Northern Hawk Owl and Bohemian Waxwing.

- With some of the most outstanding avian diversity in the United States, the Point Reyes National Seashore in California has a bird list of 470 species. Its three terrains of pastures, valleys, and forests show off everything from Tufted Puffins and Snowy Plovers to Acorn Woodpeckers.

Get to know your gulls at California's Sonny Bono Salton Sea National Wildlife Refuge, which claims 15 different species of gulls, including the rarely seen Yellow-footed Gull.

Orange County's Upper Newport Bay Ecological Reserve is home to the world's largest nesting population of Clapper Rails as well as a wintering population of Black-bellied Plovers, Red Knots, and Blue-winged Teals.

The Monte Vista Wildlife Range in Colorado is known for Sandhill Cranes in spring and fall, but it also hosts breeding Virginia Rails and Soras, a large population of ducks and waders that peaks in October, and Bald Eagles in winter.

Rocky Mountain National Park provides 13 habitats and a range of elevations for birders to enjoy. The best time to visit is June through October, and don't forget to check out the tundra, where you can spot

Golden Eagles, Northern Harriers, and White-crowned Sparrows.

Do you really need an excuse to go to Maui? Well, another can be Haleaka National Park, which has the greatest concentration of endangered birds in the United States, including several species of the Hawaiian Honeycreeper.

Deer Flat National Wildlife Refuge in Idaho offers a rare glimpse at the courtship dance and nesting life of Clark's Grebes in spring and early summer.

To see the largest concentration of nesting birds of prey in North America—including 200 pairs of Prairie Falcons—head to Idaho's Snake River Birds of Prey National Conservation Area in spring. Take any part of the 56-mile auto tour to see Northern Harriers, Ferruginous Hawks, and Golden Eagles. The museum and World Center also offer views and demonstrations with a handful of other BOP.

Hoh River Valley in Washington's Olympic National Park provides a beautiful temperate rain forest landscape in which to view Rufous Hummingbirds and Gray Jays, and to hear the song of a variety of different thrush species hiding in the surrounding Sitka spruce.

Utah's Bear River National Wildlife Refuge allows birders to stand in one spot and see American Avocet nests, Western and Clark's Grebes, waterfowl, and White-faced Ibises.

In June, Alaska's St. Lawrence Island is not to be missed. More than one million birds are flying overhead 24 hours a day. Look for Yellow-billed Loons, Horned Puffins, auklets, eiders, and Emperor Geese.

Malheur National Wildlife Refuge in Oregon offers western-rare birds during migrations, including Black-and-white and Chestnut-sided Warblers. Also look for Bullock's Orioles, Long-billed Curlews, and Ash-throated Flycatchers.

Bowdoin National Wildlife Refuge is the place to see grassland songbirds in high numbers, including the Baird's Sparrow, Sprague's Pipit, Grasshopper Sparrow, Savannah Sparrow, and Chestnut-collared Longspur—not to mentin Montana's state bird, the Western Meadowlark.

IN VINELAND, N.J., last summer, pedestrians were astonished when an English sparrow darted down from the branches of trees, alighted on their shoulders, and peered intently into their faces. Housewives were equally amazed when the same bird flew in at their open windows. It fluttered about, examined their rooms, and flew out again. The mystery grew for several days. Then the following advertisement appeared in the *Vineland Times-Journal*:

SNOBBER—SPARROW DE LUXE

BY EDWIN WAY TEALE

"Lost. Tame female English sparrow. Reward. Call 1291J."

That advertisement brought about the return of a remarkable pet. It also revealed a boy-and-bird companionship which is as interesting as it is unusual. The boy is Bennett Rothenberg; the sparrow, Snobber. They were visiting the boy's uncle near Vineland when the bird became lost.

The boy and the sparrow live on the eleventh floor of a great apartment building across from the Planetarium, on Eighty-first Street in New York City. The bird is never caged. It is free to come

and go. At will, it flies in and out of the apartment-house window more than 130 feet above the street and the Planetarium park. Each night, it sleeps on top of a closet-door left ajar near Bennett's bed.

On rainy days, the sparrow makes no effort to mount upward along the sheer cliff of brick and glass to Bennett's apartment-window. Instead, she rides up on the elevator! Flying in the front entrance of the apartment-house, Snobber alights on the shoulder of the elevator operator, Frank Olmedo. When they reach the eleventh floor, Olmedo rings the bell at the apartment and when the door opens, the sparrow flies, like a homing pigeon, to the boy's bedroom. A year ago, during a month when Bennett was away at a summer camp, Olmedo cared for the bird and the two became fast friends.

It was in the spring of 1943 that Bennett, then fourteen years old, found a baby sparrow in Central Park. He carried it home and installed it in an empty robin's nest in his room. With the aid of a medicine dropper and a pair of tweezers, he fed it at hourly intervals. On a diet of flies, bits of worms, water and pieces of eggbiscuit, it grew rapidly. It gained weight and the whitish fuzz on its body developed into scores of strong and glossy feathers.

SNOBBER—SPARROW DE LUXE

A snobbish tilt of its beak when it had had enough food gave it its name.

The boy taught Snobber to fly by placing it in low trees, offering food, and chirping to it. The sparrow now recognizes his chirp and will fly up to the apartment window from the trees below when he calls. To the uninitiated, all sparrows seem to chirp alike. But not to Bennett. He says he can recognize Snobber's chirp in a tree full of sparrows. By the sound, he can tell whether she is angry, curious, or excited. When they go for walks together, they often seem to be carrying on a conversation, chirping back and forth, as the sparrow darts ahead from tree to tree. On reaching Eighty-first Street, Snobber flies on ahead and then waits—like a dog—at the entrance of the apartment-house for Bennett to cross the street.

A friendly bird, she often is much in evidence when the boys of the neighborhood are engaged in playing games. In the middle of a baseball game, she sometimes alights on the shoulder of the batter or settles down directly on the baseline to attract attention. At other times, when the boys are flipping playing cards in local version of "pitching pennies," Snobber will dart down, grasp one of the cards in her bill, and fly away with it. Any small, shiny object

267

instantly arouses her interest. When she finds a dime on Bennett's dresser, she picks it up and darts this way and that, flying until she is tired. Two marbles in a small metal tray on the boy's desk keep her occupied for a quarter of an hour at a time. She pushes them about with her bill, apparently delighted by the jangling sound they make.

Her interest in bright-colored objects prevented Bennett, last fall, from keeping track of the position of Allied armies by means of colored pins on a large wall-map. No sooner did he put up the pins, placing them carefully to show the location of the lines, than they would disappear. He would find them lying on his bed, the dresser, his desk. Snobber, fluttering like a flycatcher in front of the map, would pull out the pins with her bill. Red-headed pins seemed her first choice with yellow-headed pins coming second. She became so interested in this game that she would perch on Bennett's shoulder, or even his hand, while he inserted the pins. Then she would pull them out as soon as he had finished his work. When he substituted tiny flags in place of pins, her interest rose to an even higher pitch. In the end, Bennett had to give up his efforts and the game ended for Snobber.

SNOBBER—SPARROW DE LUXE

One August, in Central Park, one of the eminent ornithologists of The American Museum of Natural History—a scientist who had journeyed as far away as Equatorial Africa to observe bird-life—was surprised to see something entirely new to his experience. A sparrow darted down, perched on a boy's shoulder, and began to eat ice cream from a cone. The sparrow, of course, was Snobber and the boy was Bennett.

Ice cream, pieces of apple, and small bits of candy are delicacies of which the bird is passionately fond. Boys in the neighborhood share their candy and cones with her when she alights on their shoulders. As soon as she sees a piece of candy, she begins to chirp and flutter about. Bennett and a companion sometimes play a game with her for five minutes at a time by tossing a piece of cellophane-covered candy back and forth. Like a kitten pursuing a ball, Snobber will shuttle swiftly from boy to boy in pursuit of the flying candy.

Along Eighty-first Street, pedestrians are often as surprised as were the people of Vineland to have a sparrow swoop down and alight on their shoulders. The reaction is varied. One woman jerked off a fur neck-piece and swung it around in the air like a

lasso to ward off the supposed attack. Several persons have made a grab for the sparrow. But, always, Snobber is too quick for them.

One day, last summer, an elderly gentleman, stout, near-sighted and wearing a derby hat, was walking down the Planetarium side of Eighty-first Street reading a newspaper held close to his face. In his left hand he clutched an ice cream cone from which he absent-mindedly took a bite from time to time. Snobber was perched on the lower limb of a tree. She cocked her head as he went by; she had spotted the ice cream. Swooping down, she alighted on the cone and began nibbling away. Just then, the man put the cone to his mouth abstractedly to take another bite. The cone bit him, instead! Or, at least, that was the impression he got when Snobber pecked him on the lower lip. Unable to believe his eyes, he peered near-sightedly at the cone and bird. Then he began to wave the cone in circles in the air. Like a pinwheel, the cone and the pursuing sparrow whirled above his head.

Seeing the commotion, Bennett ran across the street to explain and to catch Snobber. But in the process he accidentally knocked the cone from the man's hand. Thinking he was being set upon from the air and the ground simultaneously, the near-sighted gentleman clutched his newspaper in one hand and his derby hat in the other

and sprinted, puffing, down the street. At the end of the block, he stopped, turned, shook his fist, and hurried around the corner.

Indoors, when Snobber gets hungry she perches on a seed-box as a signal to the boy. Two of her favorite foods, aside from seeds and bits of biscuit, are cornflakes and maple sugar. She gets greens by eating pieces of leaves from time to time. If the sash is down when she wants to fly out the window, she will dash about the room in a special manner which Bennett has learned to understand.

As might be supposed, the sparrow had difficulty at first in picking out the right window among the vast number which pierce the masonry of the great apartment-house. Once, after Bennett had chirped with his head out the window he was called back into the room and when he looked out again he was just in time to see the sparrow come flying out of a window on the floor below. As a guide, he has tied a ribbon to the iron bar of a window-box outside his bedroom. Before dusk, Snobber always returns to the apartment. The only time she has spent the night outdoors was during the days when she was lost near Vineland.

From the beginning, Bennett determined that if she ever wanted to go free, he would not try to restrain her. The train-

271

trip to Vineland, last summer, was one of the few times when she has been locked in a cage. The ride was bumpy and she disliked it, chirping most of the time. Bennett spent his time during the journey explaining to interested passengers about the sparrow in the cage. At his uncle's farm, Snobber was ill at ease. She had never seen a rocking chair before and the unstable perch it provided when the boy was sitting in it, disturbed her still further.

On the second day there, she dashed from an apple tree in pursuit of two wild sparrows, flew too far, became confused, then hopelessly lost. Four days later, when Bennett recovered her through his advertisement, she was several miles from his uncle's farm in the direction of New York City. She recognized the boy in an instant and flew chirping to his shoulder. A small American flag in the window of the house where she was found resembled the ribbon tied to the window-box of the apartment-house and may have influenced her in choosing that particular place. When chasing among the trees, with wild sparrows of the Planetarium park, she seems to prefer Bennett's companionship to that of any bird. She is always slightly suspicious of other sparrows. When dusting herself with others of her kind, she always stays on the edge of the group. If one

of the birds becomes too familiar, she will charge it with lowered head and open beak. Bennett once brought home a young sparrow to keep her company. She refused to have anything to do with it. He then placed a canary in the bedroom as a playmate for Snobber. When he returned to the room to see how they were getting along, he found her holding the hapless bird by the bill and swinging it around in the air. The next day, she lured the canary out on the window-ledge and then chased it away down the street. After that, the boy ceased trying to find a bird companion for her and Snobber is well content to let matters rest as they are.

This spring, although she had not mated, Snobber was over-come by the impulse to build a nest. Tearing up a robin's nest and a song sparrow's nest, which Bennett had in his room, she used the material to create a nest of her own. She was busy with this task for days, sometimes flying about the room with straws fully a foot in length. In the nest, she laid two eggs. Neither hatched and one now rests on cotton batting in a small box which bears this notation on the lid: "English Sparrow Egg Laid By Snobber."

When Bennett is doing his homework, during winter months, Snobber often perches quietly on his book or on the desk beside

him. And, at night, when the boy is sleeping in his bed, the sparrow is lost in slumber on the top of the closet door, its head tucked in its feathers. Often, it sleeps on one leg. At such times, it has the appearance of a ball of ruffled feathers, with one leg sticking down and a tail sticking out at right angles to the leg.

As soon as it is daylight, Snobber is awake. Bennett doesn't need any alarm clock. He has Snobber. She hops down, and perches on his head, begins tugging at individual hairs. If he doesn't wake up, she often snuggles down near his neck for an additional nap herself. If he disturbs her by moving in his sleep, she gives him a peck on the chest. As a consequence, Bennett often keeps moving back toward the far side until when he wakes up he is lying on the edge and the sparrow is occupying most of the bed.

On the floor of Bennett's bedroom, there is a shiny spot six or seven inches in diameter. This is where the sparrow takes her imaginary dust-baths. Alighting at this spot, she squats down, fluffs up her feathers, turns this way and that, goes through the motions of taking a real dust-bath by the roadside.

Like Mary's famous little lamb, Snobber sometimes tries to follow Bennett to school. He rides to and from classes on the subway. Winter mornings, he always tried to leave the apartment-

house without the sparrow seeing him. But the bright eyes of the little bird miss little that is going on. Several times, just as he was sprinting into the entrance of the subway a block from his home, he has heard a lively chirping behind him and Snobber has fluttered down on his shoulder. Twice he has had to explain to teachers that he was late for classes because a sparrow delayed him! At the school he attends, however, both teachers and pupils know all about Snobber. In fact, whenever Bennett gets an extra good grade, his classmates have a standing explanation: Snobber has helped him!

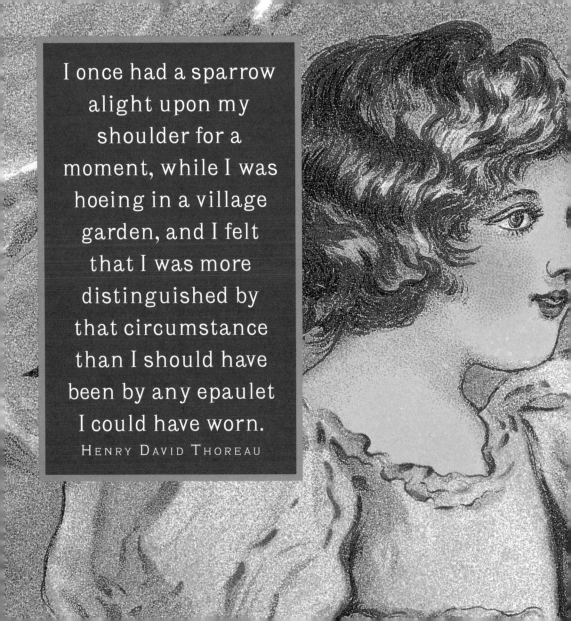

I once had a sparrow alight upon my shoulder for a moment, while I was hoeing in a village garden, and I felt that I was more distinguished by that circumstance than I should have been by any epaulet I could have worn.

HENRY DAVID THOREAU

Margaret Morse Nice

MARGARET MORSE NICE was a pioneer of behavior ornithology who took backyard bird-watching to new scientific heights. Born in 1883 in Amherst, Massachusetts, to college-educated parents, Nice was encouraged early on to develop her interest in nature. Her strong observational skills were evident as young as age 13, when she began to keep precise notes on the behavior of her sister's brown leghorn hens. This habit of detailed note-taking would help Nice change the world of ornithology some 40 years later.

Nice enrolled in Mount Holyoke College in 1901 and graduated with a bachelor of science degree five years later. She was resistant to the traditional path for educated women—living with her parents until she was married—and convinced her family to let her continue her education at Clark University. There she studied both zoology and child psychology, two subjects that deeply influenced the way in which she saw the world. In 1913, she married Clark graduate student Leonard Blaine Nice;

eventually the two moved to the University of Oklahoma, where Blaine was offered a teaching position.

By the 1920s, Blaine and Margaret had welcomed five daughters into their family. Though busy with motherhood, Nice was able to occasionally publish articles on child psychology based on the way in which her own girls related to one another. As the children grew older, Nice had more time to spend pursuing her own interests, including joining the Oklahoma Audubon Society. At a conference, she met Althea Sherman, who encouraged her to focus on her lifelong passion—ornithology. In 1924, together with her husband, Nice published a five-year study called *The Birds of Oklahoma*. But her ornithology career truly began in 1927, when the family moved to Columbus, Ohio, on the banks of the Olentangy River.

Her new home, which she dubbed Interpont, included 60 acres of scrubland. Here she began to study the nesting Song Sparrows in her own yard. By banding and watching the sparrows over several years as they returned to nest, Nice did something no other American ornithologist had done—she studied each bird as an individual. Spending thousands of hours in her yard following sparrows as they built nests and bred, Nice came

upon an undiscovered phenomenon. The sparrows—
specifically two she named Uno and 4M—engaged in
fierce territorial wars, a fact previously unknown to
ornithologists. When Nice was ready to publish her first
study on avian territoriality in breeding, the American
ornithology community was not ready to hear the work of
a "backyard birdwatcher." It took a trip overseas with her
family for her Song Sparrow studies to see publication,
first in Germany. American ornithology journals followed
in 1937 and 1943 with "Studies in the Life Histories of
Song Sparrow."

Following this seminal study, Nice dedicated 20 more
years to ornithology and conservation. She published
more than 250 articles on birds, wrote a literary
supplement to her Song Sparrow study (illustrated by
Roger Tory Peterson) titled *The Watcher at the Nest*, reviewed
more than 3,000 other works, and even assisted scientific
refugees during World War II in finding safe harbors
either in her own home or in Europe. When she passed
away in 1974, Nice had made a name for herself as *the*
backyard birdwatcher—someone who deeply believed
in the importance of nature study for scientists and
hobbyists alike.

The Hollow Wood

By Edward Thomas

Out in the sun the goldfinch flits
Along the thistle-tops, flits and twits
Above the hollow wood
Where birds swim like fish—
Fish that laugh and shriek—
To and fro, far below
In the pale hollow wood.

Lichen, ivy, and moss
Keep evergreen the trees
That stand half-flayed and dying,
And the dead trees on their knees
In dog's-mercury and moss:
And the bright twit of the goldfinch drops
Down there as he flits on thistle-tops.

Feeders!

BIRD FEEDERS are a great way to lure interesting birds into your yard, and are an important aid to all our feathered friends throughout the long summer days and the deep freeze of winter.

Suet—beef fat—is one of the best ingredients for attracting all kinds of warblers, songbirds, and migrant birds to your feeder. Remember that suet is for winter only—temperatures over 70 degrees Fahrenheit cause it to melt.

Test out these gourmet suet recipes for a livelier backyard this winter!

Suet

INGREDIENTS:

Beef fat—collect excess fat trimmed from beef cuts and store it in your freezer until you have enough, or purchase beef fat directly from the grocery store or butcher.

PREPARATION:

1. Finely chop the fat, or grind it with a meat grinder.
2. Heat the fat over a medium-low flame until it is liquefied.
3. Strain the melted suet by pouring it through a fine cheesecloth.
4. Let it cool to harden.
5. Repeat steps 2 and 3.
6. Again let the suet cool to harden, and store it in a covered container in the freezer until you're ready to use it in these fine recipes . . .

Peanut Butter Sandwich

INGREDIENTS:

1 cup fresh suet

1 cup peanut butter

3 cups yellow cornmeal

½ cup whole wheat flour

PREPARATION:

1. Melt the suet over low heat; add the peanut butter. Stir until well blended.
2. Mix together the cornmeal and flour in a large bowl.
3. Pour the suet into the dry mixture and blend thoroughly.
4. Pour or pack the mixture into a mold, feeder, or any appropriate household item (leftover mesh onion bags work great, and are easy to hang from any low branch).
5. Refrigerate or freeze until hardened.

Suet Pizza

INGREDIENTS:

2 cups suet

½ cup flour, bread crumbs, or oatmeal

Bacon drippings

Meat drippings

Peanut butter

Figs, dates, or raisins

Finely chopped apple

Seeds

PREPARATION:

1. Melt the suet over low heat; add the flour. Stir until well blended.
2. Form the mixture into a ball and roll it out flat on a greased pizza or cookie sheet.
3. Place the remaining ingredients on top.
4. Refrigerate or freeze the pizza until it's hardened, then cut it into slices. These can be set out in a suspended tray feeder.

Of course, summer is a great time for feeding as well. You'll find that a mix of seeds is best for the summer months, set out in any kind of feeder—the tube and tray feeders for sale at your local nursery work great. You can even set out specific seeds to target your favorite birds:

- Sunflower: Northern Cardinal, Black-capped Chickadee, Mourning Dove, American Goldfinch, Tufted Titmouse, Red-bellied Woodpecker.
- Corn: Red-winged Blackbird, Blue Jay, Summer Tanager, California Towhee, Common Grackle, Northern Flicker.
- Peanuts: Starlings, cardinals, juncos, finches.
- Fruit: Gray Catbird, Yellow-breasted Chat, Black-headed Grosbeak, Hooded Oriole, American Robin, Cedar Waxwing, Carolina Wren.

Make Your Own Pinecone Bird Feeder

MATERIALS:

A few feet of yarn, ribbon, or fishing wire

1 large, open pinecone

1 cup smooth peanut butter

Birdseed

PREPARATION:

1. Tie the yarn, ribbon, or wire to your pinecone about two or three layers down from the top.
2. Using a small spatula or butter knife, spread the peanut butter onto the pinecone, filling the spaces between the layers.
3. Spread the seed mixture onto a paper plate or other flat surface. Roll the peanut-buttered pinecone in seeds until it's fully covered.
4. Be sure to hang your feeder where you can see it and enjoy your visitors!

A bird does not sing because it has an answer. It sings because it has a song.

CHINESE PROVERB

The Scarlet Minivet, found throughout much of South Asia, uses scare tactics to rustle up its dinner. Living off a diet of various insects, the bird beats its wings hard and fast near foliage to frighten prey out into the light.

Birds of Asia

It takes skill and practice to mimic most birdcalls, but the Red-whiskered Bulbul, found from India through Southeast Asia, has a voice very similar to a cheerful human whistle. In fact, a human whistling into a Bulbul nest will provoke a positive reaction from young chicks.

Japanese Cranes, with their striking white plumage and black head and tail feathers, mate for life and are considered a symbol of fidelity as well as longevity and good fortune in Japan.

The Philippines are home to the Luzon Bleeding-heart, a dove that is all gray and white, with the exception of its breast, where the feathers are red and fade out into pink. Each dove has different bloodlike markings, possibly to help make individuals recognizable to the flock.

If you hear the call *oink?* while in India, it may be not a questioning pig, but rather a Plum-headed Parakeet. A green bird with a distinct plum-colored head, it's endemic to the Indian subcontinent.

Representing the war god of the Dayak people from Indonesia, the Rhinoceros Hornbill is one of the largest hornbills. The males have red or orange eyes, and both sexes have a massive upturned casque or horn on top of the beak.

The male Asian Paradise-flycatcher goes through quite a change from infancy to adulthood. Over four years, a subadult male changes from a look-alike female, with dark feathers head-to-tail, to a bird with a white body and two long tail feathers (that double its body length), which are used for courtship.

One of the world's largest birds of prey is the Philippine Eagle, and with fewer than 500 left in the wild, a conservation effort to save the "Monkey-eating Eagle" has begun. This forest-dwelling raptor, which only lays a single egg every two years, is endangered due to the harvesting of its habitat.

For beauty, look no farther than the male Mandarin Duck. With a sweeping iridescent crown, chestnut cheeks, and ornamental designs of copper, orange, olive, iridescent blue, green, and gold, he has little problem convincing his mate to return year after year.

The national bird of Nepal is the Impeyan Monal—a large mountain pheasant whose iridescent feathers of green, blue, black, and copper give it a regal air, along with crest feathers that are permanently erect on the male.

Perhaps one of the most recognizable birds of India is the Common Peafowl or Peacock. The male has approximately 150 train feathers that can be raised to a symmetrical fan for display.

The Chinese call Pheasant-tailed Jancanas "fairies walking over ripples" because their long legs, toes, and claws allow them to walk on floating water plants. These "fairies" have long tails during breeding season, when the female mates with 5 to 10 different male partners, which each takes care of incubating his clutch of eggs on his own.

Have you heard of the bird *Liocichla bugunorum*? Discovered in May 2006 by an amateur ornithologist, the multicolored bird is the first new species reported in India in more than 50 years.

291

THE NOTICE OF BIRDS by the aboriginal mind travels a curiously intricate path, taking value from association with the mysterious formless powers, as the eagle with the Thunder, twin dwellers of the upper air.

Thus eagles' plumes and bluebirds' feathers become emblems of skyey approval. Eagle down is the sign of man's secret godward aspiration, and the milky way a drift of snowy feathers where the lesser gods make prayer plumes for the elder. By association with the water-holes where they resort to feed fat on the small rodents coming to drink, snakes become water symbols, and the plumed serpent, wriggling like the lightning against the curtain of the dark cloud, the patron of the Water-Sources. There are, however, not nearly so many thick rattlers at the water-holes to-day as when our Ancients named them guardians

FROM THE LAND OF JOURNEY'S END

BY MARY AUSTIN

of the springs. Often the snake-dancers of Hopi have to make up the kiva's quota with harmless gopher-snakes, and striped frequenters of the melon fields.

I am Indian enough, I hope, not to miss the birds that are place marks; shrill, chittering Texas nighthawks above the water-holes, jewel-green hummingbirds that haunt the hundred-belled yucca bocata. Also Indian enough to leave nameless and unnoticed a hundred singers, to observe the elf owl in the sahuaro, drawing its spread wing like a lady's

293

fan, for protective cover before topaz glittering eyes....Witch, O witch...!

With this raven's plume,
With this owl's feather
I will make Black Prayers for her
Who takes my man from me. . . .
With this owl's plume
With this raven's feather!

Now and then you find a horned lark, which, like the lark that Shelley heard, rises as it sings, treasured in a cage at the pueblo, for which the children gather grasshoppers, threading them on grass stems. But for the most part it is the literary interest which is served by birds, man making them to stand for his thought in upper airy reaches of his mind, long before he had any other use for those he could not use for food. So because the track of the road-runner's feet turns two ways, he ties the shining feathers on the cradle board to confuse the evil spirits coming to trouble the child's mind, as the four-toed sign of the cross protects from harm.

Anybody who cared for birds for their own sake, however, would find all that his liking needs in the crested ranges of the Mogollon Rim, which is

the farthest north for tropic birds, and farthest south for birds of the arctic in their yearly migrations. In the Chiricahuas there is a thick-billed parrot with splashes of poppy red upon his wings, and little green macaws, whose feathers make the knot like a sprouting corn hill, tied in the dark locks of the corn-dancers, talking to themselves among the yellow pines. Or in the Alpine island tops of sacred mountains with the whistling marmot and the rabbit-eared coney, one discovers the snowy ptarmigan turning rock-moss color to protect its rock-speckled eggs, lacking all other cover between them and the sky. Between seasons, great fleets of water-fowl sail the wind rivers above the Colorado draw, or gather along the estuary, waiting for the ebb to uncover springs of sweet water among the reedy dunes, and pelicans perform their stately dance along the medanos, clotted with satin shiny clumps of *rosas San Juan*. Once the sandhill crane could be heard whooping by unfrequented watercourses, but I doubt you will hear that bugling call anywhere now except among the ghost-invoking cries of the Navajo fire-dancers, crying "Come, Come, Come!" Thus I might name a hundred species from the broad-tailed humming-birds, droning like bees about the holy peaks of San Francisco Mountains, to the hermit thrush singing at evening on steep, dark-forested slopes the sacrament of desire, only to find that for you, as for our Ancients, and Keats and Shelley, birds serve best when they serve as symbols for free roving, skyey thought.

The Eagle
By Alfred, Lord Tennyson

He clasps the crag with crooked hands;
Close to the sun in lovely lands,
Ring'd with the azure world, he stands.

The wrinkled sea beneath him crawls;
He watches from his mountain walls,
And like a thunderbolt he falls.

BIRDS IN MYTHOLOGY AND LEGEND

Birds hold a central role in the mythology of all civilizations, from ancient Egyptians to Native Americans. A bird's place in the sky has given it a magical quality, and for centuries these creatures have been revered as powerful and wise—many even believe them to serve as the connection between the soul and the afterlife. Stories of birds and birdlike creatures have explained to some the creation of the world and the redemption of the human race. Not surprisingly, birds have been used as the symbol of many of the most influential individuals, societies, and ideals throughout history.

An Inuit story explains how the loon received its trademark white "necklace" from a poor blind boy who lived with his evil grandmother. The boy tried to kill the loon at the insistence of his grandmother, but the loon was able to convince him not to. The boy then climbed on the loon's back as the loon dived three times to the bottom of the lake until the boy's eyes were clear and he could see. As a token of thanks, the boy gave the loon his only possession—a white shell necklace.

The Phoenix is present under many names in Egyptian, Chinese, and classic mythology. Best known as a bird of bright red, orange, and gold feathers, the Phoenix is the symbol of rebirth. After hundreds of years, the Phoenix builds a nest and lies in it as it catches fire; from its ashes, a new Phoenix rises.

The dove is often associated with the Persian Ishtar, the Roman Venus, and the Egyptian Isis. It is the symbol of purity, grace, and unconditional love. As with the Christian Messiah, the dove in mythology is seen as the savior of humanity.

Many ancients believed that the sun was borne aloft by eagles every morning. This has made these raptors symbols of strength, swiftness, and majesty. Eagles were so revered that they were made the sigil of the Roman Empire.

In Norse mythology, the god Odin had two indispensable companions: the Ravens Huginn and Muninn. Huginn (thought) and Muninn (memory) were sent out every morning to travel the world and gather news; they returned to Odin's shoulder at dusk.

The Thunderbird in some Native American myths was the grandson of the sky spirit who created the world. When the water spirit tried to rid the world of people by drowning out all the land, the people traveled to the highest hill and prayed. Thunderbird came to fight the water spirit,

Crows, and their Raven cousins, have always held a spot in mythology as the symbols of occult knowledge and power. Often associated with the otherworld, war, and death (perhaps from their macabre attendance on the battlefield), corvids have accompanied such mythological figures as the Greek god Apollo and the Celtic goddess Morrigan.

sending down great bolts of lightning that split open the earth—draining away the water spirit and thus saving humankind.

Ba is an ancient Egyptian word for "soul of the deceased," which appeared as a bird or a bird with a human head. The belief was that after death would come a final union between a person's body and Ba, his or her soul. Ba could fly freely over the earth, providing the mummified body in its tomb with substances necessary in the afterlife.

The Blue Jay in Chinook legend was a trickster who disobeyed his older sister—whom he was supposed to mind at all times because she was his elder. The story goes that Blue Jay's sister taught him a lesson by ordering him to marry a woman from the land of the dead and live in the underworld. When he returned to the land of the living, he was asked to cut all his hair and give it to his new father-in-law. Blue Jay refused, so he was chased by all his new male relatives until—on the verge of capture—he assumed the form of a bird and flew back to the underworld. There he remained in exile.

The Benu bird (associated with the Phoenix) was a very important avian deity of ancient Egypt, connected in mythology to three important gods: Atum, Re, and Osiris. It was said that the Benu bird flew over the water of Nun (the chaotic mass of water that preceded the earth) before creation. The bird came to rest on a rock, its cry breaking the primeval silence. This cry determined what was to be and what was not to be in the creation of the world.

Chinese mythology tells of a bird called the Jian, which had only one eye and one wing. Two Jians were thus completely dependent upon each other and inseparable, and so they came to represent the ideal partnership between husband and wife.

Jing Wei, the daughter of the ancient Chinese emperor Yan, was mercilessly drowned in the East China Sea. Her spirit was so angry that she turned into a mythical bird seeking to right this wrong. Ever since, Jing Wei has been flying back and forth from land to sea, dropping twigs and pebbles into the ocean in an effort to fill it. Legend has it that China's Jiaozhou and Shangdong peninsulas are the result of her work.

Medieval Irish court poets were responsible for recording the history and genealogy of the king they served. These accounts often took the form of poems that blended the actual history with elements of the mythological.

One king, Suibhne of Dál nAraidi, was said to be cursed by St. Ronan; he became half man and half bird, condemned to live out his life in the woods, constantly fleeing his former human companions.

On March 9, Ukrainians celebrate Strinennia, a day to invite birds (and therefore spring) to come. To do this, people bake pastries shaped like birds, and children throw them into the air. Clay images of larks are also made, their heads smeared with honey and dressed with tinsel. These are carried around the village while songs of spring are sung.

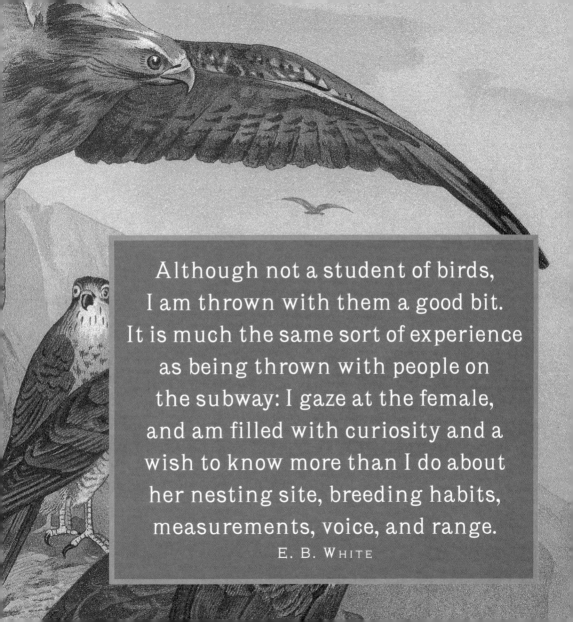

Although not a student of birds,
I am thrown with them a good bit.
It is much the same sort of experience
as being thrown with people on
the subway: I gaze at the female,
and am filled with curiosity and a
wish to know more than I do about
her nesting site, breeding habits,
measurements, voice, and range.

E. B. WHITE

YOU MIGHT BE A BIRDER IF...

ANONYMOUS

- Someone yells "Duck!" and you look up and shout "Where?"

- Vacations are planned to maximize the number of life birds.

- You criticize television programs and commercials that depict a bald eagle but play a red-tailed hawk call.

- Your kids are named Buteo and Accipiter.

- People stop and stare when you pish at the shrubbery at the local mall.

- Lunch breaks find you driving to check out your favorite hot spot.

- Your spouse says, "It's either me or the birds," and you have to think about it.

- On sunny days you hop in the car, crank up your tape of birdcalls, and drive like crazy to the nearest mountain where the thermals are great for soaring hawks.

- You pay a neighbor kid $20 to roll on a carcass and lay still while you search the sky for vultures.

- You try to talk your kid into going to college in Belize so that you have an excuse to go and bird there.

- It's a northeaster, the rain is horizontal, a small craft advisory has been issued, but it's bird-a-thon and you need to up the day's list.

- A machine squeaks at work and you describe it to maintenance as sounding like a Black-and-white Warbler.

304

- The first time you meet your future in-laws you demonstrate the courtship dance of the Woodcock, replete with sound effects.

- You spend fifteen minutes preparing dinner for your family, and thirty minutes mixing and placing seed for your birds.

- You wake up your spouse at 5:30 a.m. and exclaim, "Is that a phoebe I'm hearing outside the window?"

- Preparing for trips to visit out-of-state relatives involves contacting local birders, securing local bird lists, and buying the appropriate Lane's Guide.

- You're willing to fight with anyone who criticizes your optics.

- You participate in hours-long discussions about the pros and cons of using a certain field guide.

- You lose friends, and perhaps even your spouse, from fighting over the pronunciation of "pileated."

Pamela Rasmussen

ONE OF TODAY'S LEADING ornithologists, Pamela Rasmussen started off not unlike her predecessors from centuries past in the United States and Great Britain. At the age of eight, she discovered her unwavering passion for birds right in her own backyard. Born in a suburb of Portland, Oregon, in 1959, Rasmussen was given a junior edition of Oliver Austin's *Birds of the World* by her mother in 1967. After studying it, Rasmussen started to make connections between the birds in the book and those in the marsh just outside her back door. The thrill kick-started her professional journey.

Rasmussen attended Walla Walla College, earning a master's degree in biology in 1983, and went on to the University of Kansas, where she received a PhD in 1990 after completing her dissertation on cormorants in Patagonia. During her studies in the region, she learned how to shoot and skin birds to bring back as specimens.

Rasmussen's first job in the field was ideal, allowing her to experience a professional life similar to that her predecessors enjoyed in the 19th century: traveling, observing, collecting birds, and working with specimens in museums. Rasmussen accepted the position of assistant to S. Dillon Ripley at the Smithsonian Museum in 1992. Ripley was working to produce the definitive field guide to the avifauna of South Asia. The job offered her the chance to examine tens of thousands of the 230,000 birds native to the region that are now housed in museums around the United States, Great Britain, and India for research and display. Shortly after Rasmussen began the study, Ripley fell ill and put the responsibility of finishing the work into her hands.

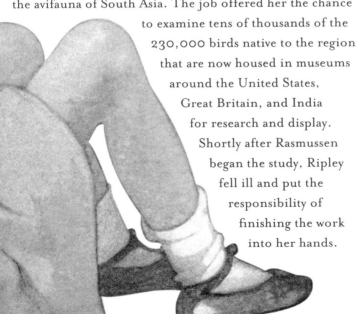

Since then, her research has taken Rasmussen on long journeys to classify South Asian birds. She has made trips to India, the Andaman Islands, Burma, and the Himalayas in search of species that had not been seen for decades, but that she wanted to be sure were extinct before excluding them from the study's findings. Her travels were not in vain: she was able to record the Serendib Sop-owl in Sri Lanka and rediscover the rare Forest Owlet in India.

When Rasmussen isn't in the field, she relies heavily on the study of skins—the preserved bodies of birds cataloged and stored in museums around the world. These historic artifacts allow scientists to study birds up close, and illustrators to reproduce their images accurately. The museums that provided Rasmussen with her specimens were the Smithsonian's Museum of Natural History, the British Natural History Museum, and the University of Michigan, where she works as the assistant curator of mammalogy and ornithology and is a visiting assistant professor of zoology.

Rasmussen has joked that she has "attention-surplus disorder," a way of describing her extreme attention to detail. Her meticulous nature led her to remeasure more than 1,000 species of already cataloged specimens. Her passion for accuracy also revealed a more disturbing side

of science when she uncovered the fraudulent acts of Richard Meinertzhagen, a now deceased soldier, spy, and bird collector. While aspects of Meinertzhagen's specimen collection had raised suspicion in the past, it was Rasmussen's digging—along with that of Robert Prys-Jones, head of the collection at the British Natural History Museum—that revealed the extent to which he had stolen specimens for the British Museum, retagged them as his own, and misrepresented their locations and migratory habits.

The culmination of Rasmussen's work is her volume *Birds of South Asia: The Ripley Guide*. Published in spring 2006, the book has been praised for bridging the gap between the recreational birder and the science of ornithology. It features detailed descriptions of birdcalls and how to recognize them, which she feels is the best starting point to identifying birds—for the seasoned ornithologist and the beginning birder alike. Pamela Rasmussen heads to Burma next on a National Geographic Society grant to the Smithsonian, where she is co-principal-investigator on a study likely to result in exciting new data—in fact, the team is hoping to encounter and study a new species of babbler that has just been discovered in the region but remains entirely unknown among humans.

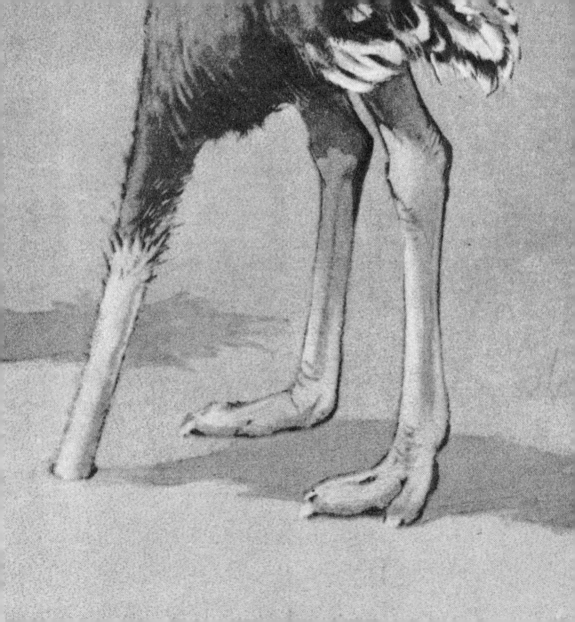

The ostrich is the world's largest and tallest bird species, with an average height of 8 feet, 2 inches. It resides predominantly in middle Africa, from Senegal to Ethiopia, and southward to Tanzania.

At 59 inches, the Goliath Heron is aptly named. This tallest and largest heron is a fascinating bird to watch while it hunts: A kink in its neck allows it to shoot straight out from a resting position with enough force to kill its prey with its beak.

Originally referred to as a whale-head, the Shoebill is named for its mammoth beak—9 inches long and 4 inches broad. This extraordinary-looking creature can be found in the marshlands of Sudan, Zambia, and Zaire.

A bird that only its mother could love is the sub-Saharan Marabou Stork. These birds have adapted to their scavenger lifestyle by developing bald heads and necks, which keep them from getting any blood or guts stuck in their feathers during mealtime.

The black-and-white Sacred Ibis resides in sub-Saharan Africa, but it was once revered farther north in ancient Egypt. There it was seen as the god of scribes, Thoth, who would often appear on earth as an ibis.

Birds of Africa

The smallest waterfowl is the African Pygmy Goose: A typical male weighs only 285 grams. Its white face and green ear patches help camouflage it in its southern Africa and Madagascar habitats, which are full of floating lilies.

A distinctive noisemaker of southern Africa is the African Fish-eagle, who has a loud, shrill, ringing cry, a sound that is often referred to as the voice of Africa.

The courtship of the Bateleur involves some of the most spectacular aerial displays a birdwatcher can see. The bird's common name is reflective of the displays, derived from the French word for "acrobat."

The Saddle-billed Stork is a stunning bird at 58 inches with black-and-white feathers. Perhaps its most striking feature is its long crimson beak, which has a black stripe and a yellow shield across the top.

Standing 3 feet tall, the Secretary Bird is an unusual bird of prey. It rarely flies, having developed strong legs for running in grassland and long tail feathers to balance it.

The national bird of Uganda is the Gray Crowned-crane, which has a spiky crest and red throat wattle. It is the most primitive member of its family, Gruidae, dating back to the Eocene period.

The Gray Parrot is a very popular house pet known for its linguistic abilities, but you can see it in the wild throughout tropical West Africa in lowland forests and mangroves.

The bird family Musophagidae is found throughout Africa. The Great Blue Turaco, White-bellied Go-away-bird, Red-crested Turaco, and Schalow's Turaco all have unique and magnificent crests.

For display plumage, look no farther than the male Standard-winged Nightjar. A large feather grows out of the middle of each wing; together, they resemble two flags flying above the bird.

In tropical Africa, if you look hard, you might see what seems to be a small gray mouse clinging to branches. It may be a Blue-naped Mousebird, which has long gray tail feathers and four toes that can all point forward to help the bird perch.

If you see a few adult Greater African Flamingos with many young flamingos, those might not be the parents—they could be the babysitters! Some of these adult birds commonly stay behind to watch the young while the others go off on feeding trips.

SOUTH
AFRICA

There is symbolic as well as actual
beauty in the migration of the birds...
There is something infinitely healing
in the repeated refrains of nature—the
assurance that dawn comes after
night, and spring after winter.

RACHEL CARSON

I AM ALONE on the hotel roof, the first time I have been alone for over a week. That's why I mounted the stairs to the sixth-floor rooftop hawk-watch before seven o'clock. I am seeking quiet time for contemplation and perspective.

TO DRINK FROM A RIVER, TO SWIM IN THE MILKY WAY

A MIRACULOUS RIVER OF RAPTORS FLOWS OVER VERACRUZ

BY CLAY SUTTON

The vista is a study in gray, the rain-laden gulf clouds hanging low over the ocean to the east, blocking the morning sun and muting the verdant tropical tones. Pico de Orizaba, Mexico's highest peak, nearly seventy-five miles to the west, is visible, though, its snow-covered slopes bathed in sunlight and shining through the humid coastal clouds. The volcano is distant, dormant, but dominant. It brings to mind prehistoric days, when nature more visibly controlled our planet. It's only the second time I've seen the mighty mountain, and I wonder if it could be an omen, a portent of good fortune for the last day of our tour.

TO DRINK FROM A RIVER, TO SWIM IN THE MILKY WAY

I discover I have company. The local peregrine, probably wintering here now, sits atop the radio tower across the street, nearly eye level and scope-close. I see it preen, then sleepily close its eyes, dreaming perhaps of its arctic aerie or maybe fat Latin pigeons. A Yellow-throated Warbler forages in a palm tree in the city park below, seemingly way out of place to one who is more used to seeing Yellow-throated Warblers on their now-distant breeding grounds, in the pines at Jakes Landing, just a few miles from my New Jersey home.

The city of Cardel, Veracruz, is slowly rousing. The smells begin to drift up, invisible tendrils wafting over the parapet, a uniquely tropical blend of wood-fire smoke, frying foods, fresh produce, and pastries. Later in the day, the Latino bustle—noise, music, horns, unmuffled engines—may perhaps be hard to reconcile with the tranquil beauty of the farmlands and sugarcane fields beyond the city, but now, early, it all blends together into a background hum easy on the mind. On transmission towers beyond the edge of town, Black Vultures and spread-wing Turkey Vultures festoon the girders, awaiting the sun, or thermals, or perhaps just waiting.

TO DRINK FROM A RIVER, TO SWIM IN THE MILKY WAY

The sky is blue to the west, but a cloud bank hovers in the east, threatening. The wind is from the south; the air seems to be thickening. Being from the east coast of the United States, I automatically assume there needs to be a northwest wind to trigger fall raptor migration. I begin to fret. Will they come today? Almost all of the world's Broad-winged Hawks pass over Cardel, but the big flight hasn't occurred yet. It's overdue. It's October 3, prime time, indeed *peak* time, but for me, for us, it's now or never—today is our last day here, the final day of our bird tour. We missed the big flight last year. Will that happen again? If so, it won't be "you should have been here yesterday" but "you should have been here tomorrow."

The city fully awakens. Cars and trucks loaded with people ply the streets below. Volkswagen taxis whiz around in all directions. Bus horns blare. The birds awaken, too. Red-billed Pigeons streak over, a small flock of Aztec Parakeets clatters by. Noisy, grating Great-tailed Grackles litter the town square. The sad calls of caged birds filter up from beneath red tile roofs.

The first kettle is right overhead, low, point-blank, although I somehow never see it coming. About fifty Broad-winged Hawks and nearly thirty Swainson's Hawks—more Swainson's than we've seen all week, a good sign. Scanning reveals flocks forming, hawks getting up out of the trees, swirling low to the north of town. Will it happen? Is it happening? Please, please, please...

Now the flocks, though still small, are advancing, coming on and over as steady as the waves on the nearby beach. As rising morning thermals falter, the birds stream, heading due south, streaming in legions, looking for the next kettle forming over an altitude-gaining thermal. For a broadwing, migration is deceptively simple: convert altitude to speed, speed to distance—distance that stretches from Canada to South American cloud forests.

I am no longer alone. The hawk-counters arrive and comment on how early the flight has begun. They speculate that this might be "the big one." The official count begins at nine, and such is the scale, the enormity, of the Veracruz flight that there is little concern that the counters might have already missed maybe a thousand birds.

320

The distant waiting vultures stir, flapping, struggling initially, then locking their wings and joining the whirling uplifted kettle. The sun breaks through, the lambent light cutting the humid haze to reveal kettles stretching to the western horizon, to the base of the hills that constrict the flyway. Our group and others arrive on the roof and marvel, some loudly, some quietly and personally. I scan 360 degrees and do a quick count. I estimate that 22,000 broadwings are now in sight at once. A veteran raptor biologist tells me that my guess is too low.

The miraculous flight begins to shift inland as the south wind turns east, causing the flocks and lingering clouds to drift away from the coast and our rooftop vantage point. We hastily arrange to move. When we hit the street, the city din crashes like thunder. I realize, dumbly, that it wasn't that we hadn't heard it, couldn't hear it, six flights up, but that the clamor had simply disappeared, fallen away while we were lost in the world above. I recall one time in southeastern Arizona's "sky island" mountains when fog and clouds cloaked the vast valleys below, the peaks becoming islands in an ocean of mist. This was similar, the hotel rooftop a quiet island in the roiling sea below. As we board the taxis, above the noise I hear the still-perched peregrine chatter a challenge at another passing Peregrine Falcon as it rushes by, streaking south.

We race inland, trying to get back underneath the flow, arriving at Chichicaxtle, eleven kilometers inland, about fifteen minutes later. The town of "Chichi" is the auxiliary count site, used when gulf-effect east winds push flights west of the Hotel Bienvenido and downtown Cardel. We erupt from the cars onto a schoolyard soccer field, dodging not only soccer balls, but a gamboling, galloping donkey, too. Looking up, we are awed, dumbstruck. Broadwings now stretch from horizon to horizon, from the east from whence we came to as far west as we can see. The advancing streams of birds extend back into infinity against the blue cloud-shrouded hills in the north.

I begin to realize that despite twenty-five years of hawk-watching I am unprepared for this event. I have seen several flights of maybe 10,000 broadwings in Texas and enjoyed at least two 10,000-plus days at Cape May. And the previous year, we witnessed a 149,000-hawk day at Cardel. But that flight had been high, protracted—manageable.

322

TO DRINK FROM A RIVER, TO SWIM IN THE MILKY WAY

I am now hard-pressed to comprehend the enormity,
the magnitude of this passage. It defies logic. I have always
been able to enumerate, to pigeonhole, a flight, but now I am
simply overwhelmed. The hawk-counters, mostly silent under
the pressure of the siege, nevertheless take the time to tell us
"We just counted twenty thousand in sight at once." Twenty
thousand. More than an entire season at most major hawk-
watches, a lifetime's supply at lesser ones. Accordingly, there is
little to measure the Cardel flight by, no yardstick that works.

So we don't even try to count. We just watch, awestruck,
looking up in open-mouthed wonder at the incomprehensible
journey above. With writing in mind, I try to think of ways
to describe it. But it's like trying to photograph the Grand
Canyon—largely impossible. I have a passing thought of a
living, moving erector set, for each kettle is connected to
others by streams of hawks, a vast matrix high overhead, like
a sky-full of molecular diagrams.

The vast streams converge and coalesce, coagulating into
kettles. The birds then circle endlessly, gradually rising.
Finally, as the thermal dies, they stream again, heading for the
next signpost, a kettle marking a column of upward-flowing

air. The kettles themselves are vast vortices, tornadoes of hawks snaking up into the sky. Because the clouds have remained, most birds are silhouettes, yet all are low. The counters would later say that it is rare, indeed almost unique, to have such a big flight so low, so point-blank overhead. The birds may not be struggling, but because of the cloud cover, warmth and resultant thermal lift is precious, and the birds spend an inordinate amount of time circling before streaming south. The kettles are like pitchers filling with water. The level rises from the bottom, overflowing the top when the pitcher can hold no more. I focus on a specific point in the middle of a kettle without moving my binoculars. It's like looking through a child's kaleidoscope at a shifting, swirling pattern of raptors.

As the blizzard of birds covers the sky, we marvel, yet in the way of humans, or at least biologists, we try to describe it. Tom Wood, here with his wife, Sheri Williamson, both on busmen's holidays from their jobs as codirectors of the Southeastern Arizona Bird Observatory, say it best: "It's like looking at a galaxy of hawks, a Milky Way of birds." Indeed stargazing is the only time in my life I have seen so many objects in the sky.

324

It's soon past noon, and the passage continues. We are almost giddy now. Ridiculous thoughts come. I laughingly wonder if the team of counters ever needs oil for their clickers or to throw water on them to cool them off. Then I'm troubled by the thought that they might develop carpal tunnel syndrome from the clicking. Raptor-induced CTS. One broadwing flies upstream, resolutely flapping north. What's up with that? Sheri quips, "He forgot his keys." As a particularly low and orderly group of hawks skims by, Sheri says, "God, I love a parade!"

The pageant continues unabated. Our Pronatura colleagues (from the dedicated premier Mexican conservation group, who study, count, and protect the migration) have termed the world's largest hawk flight *El Rio de Rapaches*, "The River of Raptors." I now understand why. Flocks of birds stretch from horizon to horizon as they come from the north and flow to the south. The river is now cresting, overflowing its banks. It's at flood stage.

Mid-afternoon. The clouds continue, but it is the warmest part of a tropical day. Some hawks are in high streams, traveling much farther between kettles. There is more time to appreciate the variety. High Ospreys, wings set, push south. Here a Cooper's Hawk, there an American Kestrel, yonder several Mississippi Kites. A high Zone-tailed Hawk masquerades among the Turkey Vultures, and a paddle-winged Hook-billed Kite contrasts sweetly with the slender Swainson's and Broad-winged hawks.

The afternoon brings a push of waterbirds. Flocks of Wood Storks appear, mostly in loose Vs, flapping more than soaring. Distant gooselike strings materialize into vast flocks of White Pelicans, first wheeling in unison, flashing brilliant white against blue-gray skies, then peeling off into ever-changing lines as the strings cross. It's as if they are trying to spell out something in a language not yet learned, a cipher understood only by pelicans. Overhead, lines of Anhingas, gangly, prehistoric, glide silently amongst the broadwings.

It's close to three p.m., and the flight endures unchecked. After seven hours, the movement has become almost mind-numbing. At one point I become disoriented, spatially confused by all the converging, diverging flocks. The discomfiture leads to a temporal drift; the magnificent journey in the sky harkens back to earlier times, to a less embroiled, threatened earth, a primal planet. I experience an overwhelming sensation that this is the way it should be, a conviction that this is right. I try to shake off the disorientation; I attribute it to lack of sleep, a hectic schedule, the end of a long tour. I try to refocus but then realize that it is more than that; deep feelings are welling up.

I walk off, leaving the group, and wander over to the other side of the now-quiet soccer field. As a raptor enthusiast, I had always wanted to see "the big flight," to experience not only the river but a flood. I had always wondered how long it would take, how many years, if ever. I had come so close so many times, at Hawk Mountain, Santa Ana, Duluth, Braddock Bay. The realization that this was *it* hit hard; the drama of the life above sobered me. I stood apart, and tears filled my eyes. It wasn't so much that I couldn't speak, I just couldn't think of the words. It was the first time in my life I'd ever walked away from a tour I was leading, but at that moment I needed to be alone.

Back home in New Jersey, I'm an active naturalist, plying the woods a fair share of the time, probably more than most. This summer past I knew of just two local pairs of broadwings, and the thousand or so that pass Cape May each year are but a trickle, a tiny tributary to the raptor river flowing over Veracruz. That more than 1.7 million broadwings pass over Cardel each fall is more than a spectacle, it's a miracle, a testament. It shows just how vast the eastern North American forests are—so large that they can produce this unfathomable number of broadwings. Such thoughts are restorative: that the United States and Canada can still produce this vast wealth of creatures at the top of the food chain, that South America can still absorb and nurture them in winter as our northern forests sleep. There is a message of hope in this massive broadwing flight. As long as there is a pure and free-flowing river of raptors, maybe the problems of the planet are not insurmountable. Maybe at least there's still time.

Much later that evening, after hours of compilation, the Pronatura hawk-counters relax in the Hotel Bienvenido's street-side cafe, drinking celebratory *cervezas*. The sound of a gentle tropical rain mixes with mariachi music, muting the drone of the traffic. The biologists give us the news: the official count for the day is nearly 500,000 broadwings. They also say that the flight was so large and broad-fronted that they probably missed at least part of it. It boggles the mind to know that they have had single-day counts of over one million birds at Cardel, Veracruz. It is incomprehensible to imagine a flight twice as large as that day's.

I've not seen the great bison herds on the American plains as they moved beneath endless flocks of Passenger Pigeons darkening prairie skies. Nor has anyone in our time. Nor will anyone ever again. It will take another planet, another heaven and earth, for that to occur. I have never seen the great plains of the Serengeti, and I have yet to see the enormous seabird flights above the Bering Sea. I hope to, someday. But I have been privileged to see green Mexican mountains turn orange with winter Monarch Butterflies, and I've shared the arctic tundra with vast herds of Caribou migrating across the north slope of Alaska's magnificent Brooks Range. And now I've quenched my thirst for hawks, nourished by the River of Raptors that flows uninterrupted down Veracruz's lush coast. These visions speak to me, to us, of what the Passenger Pigeons must have been like in their multitudes. They are visions of the past, and yet of a possible future. In Veracruz, immersed in a swirl of hawks, I now know what it's like to drink from a river and to swim in the Milky Way.

The town of San Blas, 80 miles north of Puerto Vallarta on the Pacific Ocean, offers a variety of places to bird, including mangrove, swamps, shrimp ponds, lagoons, and the shores of Rio San Cristóbal. Make sure you give yourself a week for this birder's getaway.

Birding in Mexico and the Caribbean

Take the Chihuahua–Pacific railway through Copper Canyon along Chihuahua state's Sierra Madre Occidental for spectacular views and birdwatching. Canyon avians include such Mexican endemics as the Lilac-crowned Parrot and Military Macaw, as well as residents like Berylline Hummingbirds and Tufted Flycatchers.

Sierra Gorda Biosphere Reserve is the most ecologically diverse protected area in Mexico. It covers the northern third of the state of Querétaro, with ecosystems that range from semidesert to cloud forest. This diversity enables more than 360 bird species to live there.

In October, experience the natural phenomenon of the "River of Raptors" in Veracruz, where single-day counts have exceeded 700,000 hawks, and the one-day record is 1.5 million!

Mexico City's population may exceed 20 million, but it, too, has some great opportunities for birdwatchers. The University Botanic Gardens offers endemics such as the Ocellated Thraser and Blue Mockingbird. For those looking for more of an adventure, head to Contreras Valley, a wooded area in southwest Mexico City. The valley provides a home for endemics including the White-striped Woodcreeper and Aztec Thrush.

Isla Raza in Baja California is a small island, but it is the breeding location for 90 percent of the world's Elegant Terns. Take a boat from Bahía de Los Angeles and enjoy Heerman's Gulls, boobies, and Royal Terns.

Cozumel is an island off the shore of Yucatán, easily reachable by airplane from the United States. Its name literally translates to "land of swallows," but you'll be able to see plenty of other avian life too,

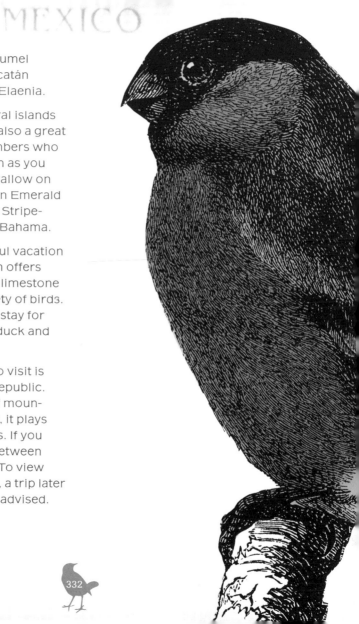

including the endemic Cozumel Emerald, as well as the Yucatán Parrot, and the Caribbean Elaenia.

The Bahamas boasts several islands with excellent birding. It's also a great place for those family members who would rather focus on a tan as you search out the Bahama Swallow on New Providence, the Cuban Emerald on Abaco, or the Northern Stripe-headed Tanager on Grand Bahama.

Aside from being a beautiful vacation destination, Grand Cayman offers wetlands, mangroves, and limestone woodlands that suit a variety of birds. Come for the beaches and stay for the West Indian Whistling-duck and Cuban Bullfinch!

One of the hottest places to visit is currently the Dominican Republic. With breathtaking vistas of mountains, beaches, and forests, it plays host to 28 endemic species. If you want to see warblers, go between mid-March and mid-April. To view more of the endemic birds, a trip later in the spring or summer is advised.

332

After taking in the Dominican Republic, many birders continue on to Puerto Rico, where they can see all the key birds in just a few days. These include the beloved Elfin-woods Warbler and White-tailed Tropicbird.

A tried-and-true Caribbean birding spot is definitely Jamaica, with 28 endemic species and a staggering list of Caribbean and near endemics as well. Check out the areas of Rocklands near Montego Bay, Cockpit Country, or the wooded Marshall's Pen in south-central Jamaica for the best birding.

St. Lucia in the Lesser Antilles is another popular vacation spot that also boasts a rugged terrain with volcanic peaks, and birds such as the St. Lucia Parrot, Black Finch, and Nightjar.

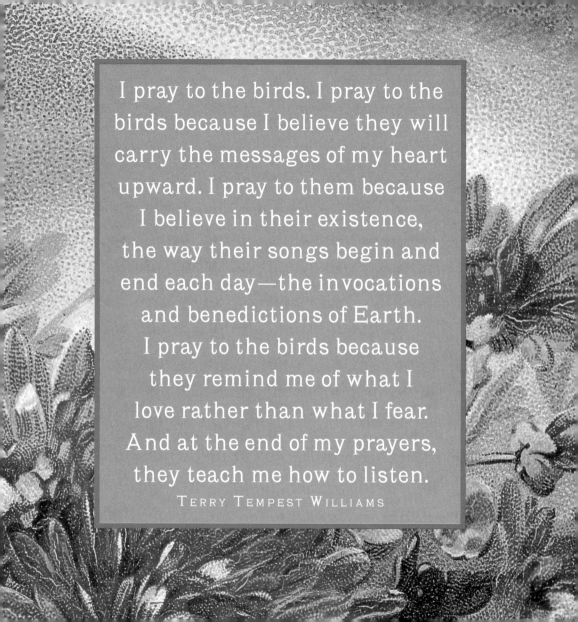

I pray to the birds. I pray to the birds because I believe they will carry the messages of my heart upward. I pray to them because I believe in their existence, the way their songs begin and end each day—the invocations and benedictions of Earth. I pray to the birds because they remind me of what I love rather than what I fear. And at the end of my prayers, they teach me how to listen.

TERRY TEMPEST WILLIAMS

ENDANGERED BIRDS

As our world becomes more and more crowded, it's only natural that ecosystems continually change. However, the declining populations of bird species we're currently experiencing are not natural. Sadly, due mostly to human interference, we are losing many important species every year. Dwindling numbers result from many factors, but the phenomena that account for most are deforestation, agriculture, hunting, draining of wetlands, the exotic bird pet trade, and household pets. Visit your local zoo, nature conservatory, or birding society to learn what you can do to foster the populations of the native birds in your area!

Ivory-billed Woodpecker:
Deforestation in the southeastern United States caused the decline of this big woodpecker because each pair requires up to 10 square miles of lowland forest to survive. The last confirmed sightings were in the 1940s in Louisiana and the 1950s in Cuba, but unconfirmed reports have continued right up to the present. Credible sightings in Arkansas in 2004 led to a massive search, but no one was able to photograph or otherwise document an Ivory-bill there.

Eskimo Curlew: The Eskimo Curlew was aggressively hunted in the 1800s on its migration path from northwest Canada to South America, and has been ravaged by predation and disease since. There are still possible sightings reported occasionally, but the last definite records of Eskimo Curlew sightings were in the 1960s.

California Condor: In 1982, after 25 years on the endangered species list, fewer than two dozen California Condors remained in the wild. Mating condor pairs produce only one egg every two years, but due to an intense captive breeding program, their wild population has since increased to 83, while 137 remain in captivity. California Condors have a wingspan of better than 9 feet, allowing them to soar more than 100 miles a day searching for food.

Yellow-crested Cockatoo: The main factor responsible for the Yellow-crested Cockatoo's rapid decline has been the exploitation of the species for the pet trade. With its dramatic yellow crest and white body feathers, this species is found now only in the central archipelagos of Indonesia and East Timor.

Black-capped Vireo: This warbler-size vireo was once widespread from Mexico to Kansas, but due to human factors—development, fire suppression, agriculture—the small population is now limited to Texas and a small section of Oklahoma. Audubon Texas has begun collaborating with the Environmental Defense Fund on the innovative Landowner Conservation Assistance Program, which encourages private landowners to help Black-capped Vireos and other endangered species in the Texas Hill Country.

Kirtland's Warbler: Commonly referred to as the Jack Pine Warbler, Kirtland's nest on the ground under living jack pine branches. Currently, the population nests in a few counties in Michigan's Lower

Peninsula, in addition to a few pairs that can be found in Wisconsin, Ontario, and the Upper Peninsula. Due to the Kirtland's unique nesting requirements, scientists believe it has always been rare. Population surveys are conducted annually by counting the songs of the male warblers, which are distinct, loud, and melodious, and can be heard at a distance of a quarter mile.

Florida Scrub Jay: This blue beauty calls the high, dry habitat of the Florida scrub its only home. The scrub occurs in small patches across the state and hosts dozens of plant and animal species that occur nowhere else in the world. Unfortunately, these areas are also very desirable to developers and citrus growers, and their appropriation of this land—bringing with them pesticides, busy roads, and house pets—has contributed significantly to the declining jay population.

Marbled Murrelet: This seabird is found along the western coast of North America, from the Bering Sea to central California. Unlike most seabirds, the murrelet can nest up to 45 miles inland, often in the old-growth forests of the Pacific Northwest. When not nesting, the birds live at sea and feed close to the shore. Deforestation is the most significant

factor in the decline of the species. Pacific Lumber Company, which owns some of the last old-growth California redwood stands, has agreed to a habitat conservation plan in collaboration with state and federal government in an attempt to preserve what is left of the population.

Humboldt Penguin: These small-in-stature penguins are big on noise, being well known for their raucous, braying calls; they've lived on the coast of Chile and Peru for thousands of years. In the last century, however, their droppings have been harvested for fertilizer, resulting in serious damage to their habitat. Today only about 10,000 survive.

Whooping Crane: In the late 1800s, there were about 1,500 whooping cranes living in the aspen parkland and prairie regions of western Canada and the United States as human settlement spread westward. The world population dropped to as low as 14 to 16 living cranes in the 1940s. In November 2006, biologists with the U.S. Fish and Wildlife Service counted a total of 234 Whooping Cranes, the highest number since the government began taking censuses. Whooping Cranes live up to 24 years in the wild, and mate with one partner for life.

The Wild Swans at Coole

By William Butler Yeats

The trees are in their autumn beauty,
The woodland paths are dry,
Under the October twilight the water
Mirrors a still sky;
Upon the brimming water among the stones
Are nine-and-fifty swans.

The nineteenth autumn has come upon me
Since I first made my count;
I saw, before I had well finished,
All suddenly mount
And scatter wheeling in great broken rings
Upon their clamorous wings.

I have looked upon those brilliant creatures,
And now my heart is sore.
All's changed since I, hearing at twilight,
The first time on this shore,
The bell-beat of their wings above my head,
Trod with a lighter tread.

Unwearied still, lover by lover,
They paddled in the cold
Companionable streams or climb the air;
Their hearts have not grown old;
Passion or conquest, wander where they will,
Attend upon them still.

But now they drift on the still water,
Mysterious, beautiful;
Among what rushes will they build,
By what lake's edge or pool
Delight men's eyes when I awake some day
To find they have flown away?

Frank M. Chapman

FRANK MICHLER CHAPMAN was born in Englewood, New Jersey, in 1864. In his 81 years, Chapman would make a huge impact on the world of ornithology, amateur birdwatching, and conservation. Though he would eventually be considered the Dean of American Ornithologists, Chapman took his time letting the passion for birds take hold. As a young boy, he was drawn to birdsongs, referring to them as "Nature's most eloquent expression." After graduating from Englewood Academy in 1880, however, he chose a practical career as a banker at the American Exchange National Bank in New York City.

Chapman spent his weekends and vacations on bird-related trips and also participated in local bird counts with the US Bureau of Biological Survey. By 1886, he could no longer deny his interest and quit the bank to pursue birds full time. With only a high school education, Chapman headed south to Florida where he worked with an independent investigator, returning with a collection of birds. With the permission of the American Museum of Natural History in New York, Chapman spent time comparing his birds with the institution's vast

collection. Under the guidance of two more experienced ornithologists, Chapman gained vital insight into the world of museums and foreign birds. A year later, the museum hired him as the assistant to Dr. J. A. Allen, the head of the Department of Mammals and Birds.

Chapman's keen interest helped him rise quickly in the organization, moving to assistant curator, then associate curator; in 1920, when the Department of Birds became its own domain, he became curator, a position he held until his retirement in 1942. His work at the museum deeply impacted modern research on South American birds, as well as how the public viewed the avian displays at the museum. In 1902, Chapman opened the first-ever exhibit whose dioramas focused exclusively on birds in their habitats. He set the precedent for the now famous American Museum dioramas by visiting each site chosen for depiction with a team of artists and scientists. An early conservationist, he also concentrated on birds and animals threatened by extinction.

A prolific lecturer and writer of field guides and magazine articles, he called for better awareness of of habitat and animal conservation. In 1900, he proposed a new event to counter a tradition called the Christmas Side Hunt, in which hunters competed to shoot as many birds as possible. With Chapman's inspiration, 27 birders—based everywhere

from Toronto to California to New York—participated
in the world's first Christmas Bird Count. The tradition
continues to this day, with 50,000 birders a year now
engaging in this crucial early-winter population census.

Also during this period, Chapman—with the aid of the
newly formed Audubon Society—founded a journal in which
young birders could publish their findings as well as be
guided by more experienced ornithologists. *Bird-Lore*, as it was
called, was edited by Chapman from 1899 until 1934 when
he sold it to the society. It was eventually renamed *Audubon*.

When he retired from the museum, Chapman and
his family moved south so that he could focus on his study
of a bird's place in nature year-round. He became a huge
supporter of Barro Colorado Island, with his enthusiasm
helping establish this spot as an esteemed center for
tropical research.

When he passed away in 1945, Chapman had traveled
the world pursuing his passion and was the recipient of
numerous awards and honors including the Roosevelt
Medal, the first Elliot Medal, and the first Linnaean Society
Medal. He was considered a kind mentor, and visitors to
the American Museum of Natural History can still witness
his commitment to birds in the Frank M. Chapman Hall of
North American Birds.

Bird Conservation

SO YOU'VE BECOME pretty fond of the little creatures you see flitting around your backyards and local nature centers. You've created a birdbath and planted a bird-friendly garden, and you've been studying the vireos in your field guide closely. That's all there is to the birding thing, right? It can be, but if you appreciate birds today, consider getting active in bird conservation to guarantee that future generations will be able to enjoy them, too!

The British essayist Robert Lynd (1879–1949) once said, "There is nothing in which the birds differ more from man than the way in which they can build and yet leave a landscape as it was before." Evidence of this is clear everywhere around us. As we continue to develop and expand our cities and towns, more and more natural habitats are being damaged, and pollution levels are rising. Though some birds can happily survive in these new urban landscapes, others are much more dependent on large areas of grassland or woodland—and migrating birds often need two or more specific environments throughout their travels in order to survive. It's up to us nature lovers to keep those environments intact and healthy!

348

HERE ARE A FEW SIMPLE WAYS TO HELP:

Keep up that backyard habitat. Your bird feeder or birdhouse can do wonders in providing homes for migrating, breeding, or local birds. When working on your yard, try to find alternatives to chemical pesticides. And if you have a large wooded lot, make an effort to keep around as much dead plant material as is safe—fallen limbs and leaves provide great spots for birds to find tasty insect treats!

Writing a letter can still make an impact. Whether directed to elected officials, neighborhood organizations, or the editors of your local paper, letters go a long way toward conservation if they are done right. Make sure to write in clear and concise language, and try to address a specific bill or local event. Connect the issue with how it will affect not just you and your fellow birdwatchers, but the general population as well. And finally—if you can—provide a solution. People respond to positive alternatives!

Volunteer for a Christmas Bird Count in your area, or offer to take groups of aspiring young birders out to learn about nature. Ask at your local nature center or Audubon Club—they'll be thrilled to suggest any upcoming ways to help your area birds.

You can find more great ideas online at the American Bird Conservancy (www.abcbirds.org), Cornell Lab of Ornithology (www.birds.cornell.edu), Audubon Watch List (www.audubon.org/bird/watch), and US Fish and Wildlife Service Division of Bird Habitat Conservation (www.fws.gov/birdhabitat).

How can hope be denied when there is always the possibility of an American Flamingo or a Roseate Spoonbill floating down from the sky like pink rose petals?

TERRY TEMPEST WILLIAMS